It was so important to look great. Surely her mom would understand.

"READ THIS!" TESS REACHED INTO HER FANNY PACK AND TOOK out the modeling-school paper.

Her mom read over the paper. Tess watched her face, looking for a smile, a frown, anything. But nothing crossed her mom's face.

"It looks interesting," she finally said.

Uh-oh.

"We saw some of the girls doing their modeling assignment today at the mall. It looked really cool and fun, and a lot of great things could happen like new clothes and modeling afterward. Erin and I really want to sign up." The words tumbled out like a waterfall. "Is that okay?"

Tess left off the part about how she already had told Miss Wakested they would be there Monday.

Secret Sisters: (se´-krit sis´-terz) n. Two friends who choose each other to be everything a real sister should be: loyal and loving. They share with and help each other no matter what!

Secret ✼ Sisters

Picture Perfect

Sandra Byrd

WATERBROOK
PRESS

PICTURE PERFECT
PUBLISHED BY WATERBROOK PRESS
2375 Telstar Drive, Suite 160
Colorado Springs, Colorado 80920
A division of Random House, Inc.

Scriptures in the Secret Sisters series are quoted from the *International Children's Bible, New Century Version,* copyright © 1986, 1988 by Word Publishing, Nashville, TN 37214. Used by permission.

The characters and events in this book are fictional, and any resemblance to actual persons or events is coincidental.

ISBN 1-57856-063-2

Published in association with the literary agency of Janet Kobobel Grant, Books & Such, 3093 Maiden Lane, Altadena, CA 91001.

Printed in the United States of America
2000—First Edition

10 9 8 7 6 5 4 3 2 1

To Robin Jones Gunn,
a beautiful person, inside and out

one

We'll Be There—for Sure

Saturday Afternoon, July 5

Tess pushed back the clothes on the rack. None of these would look good on her. Now if she looked like Erin, she would have found ten outfits.

"Ready to go?" Erin, her best friend and Secret Sister, came up alongside her holding a cute shorts set.

Tess stepped back from the clothing display. Erin probably knew what size Tess wore, but she was still embarrassed.

"Yeah." Tess checked her watch. "My mom said if I was late I was never coming to the mall alone again."

They rushed across the junior department, trying to find a place to pay for Erin's clothes. A herd of impatient buyers crowded the nearest counter.

"A different cashier?" Erin asked.

"Sure," Tess said. They kept looking, but the crowds grew even thicker. A stream of people lined both sides of the store's center aisle like a crowd parting for a parade.

"What are they all doing here? It looks like they're watching something," Erin said.

Tess looked at the clock on the wall. "Well, we *do* have nine minutes to get to the mall exit. Let's check it out!"

The store walls were lined with pink and purple. A neon cactus glowed from above them with a desert sunset scene painted in the distance. Tess and Erin made their way to the center of the aisle where a girl about their age modeled an awesome outfit.

"And this is the new navy blue sailor sweater with the latest jeans from Gloria," the announcer's buttery voice called out. "Paired with blue leather clogs from the shoe department downstairs." The model walked off to the side where a man sat in a huge chair, watching the models and flipping through pictures.

"That was a cool outfit," Tess said. "It would look great on you." If only she looked as good as Erin—as good as almost anyone else, really—instead of disappearing into the background wherever she went.

"Thanks." Erin nodded. "Look, here comes another one."

Tess watched as the girl, who also seemed to be about twelve years old, walked down the center of the row. She modeled a pair of khakis with a silky, tucked-in shirt the color of a peach.

"That would look so good on you," Erin said.

Tess stared at the model. "Do you think so? I always think I look weird if I try anything dressy like that shirt."

Erin nodded. "It would look great."

Maybe it *would*. But Tess hadn't seen it on the racks, and she was sure she had looked through the whole junior section. Everything she had tried on had made her look like a dumpling or a field mouse. Junior high was just around the corner. She needed help *now*.

"Your mom will be here really soon," Erin said. "Let's go pay."

Tess watched the latest model leave the aisle and step to the side with the rest of the crowd. "You go pay," Tess said. "I'm going to talk with that model."

"You're going to *what?*"

"I'm going to talk with that model, you know, just for a second. While you're paying. It won't take any extra time, don't worry! I didn't see that outfit anywhere, and I kind of like it. I might put it on hold till I can come back with my mom."

Erin shook her head. "Okay, crazy." She smiled. "I'll meet you at the checkout stand."

Tess swallowed over a dry spot in her throat as she worked her way over to where the girl stood. Talking to that model had seemed like a good idea, but as every step took Tess a little closer, she wasn't so sure. The girl in the peach-colored shirt stood to the side of the crowd, watching another model. Tess finally positioned herself next to her and breathed in the light rose-water scent of her perfume.

"Um, excuse me," Tess croaked out. Nobody heard her. Not even the girl she was talking to.

One more try, then she would scurry away!

"Um, excuse me," she said, a little louder, voice quivering.

"Are you talking to me?" Peachy Girl said.

Why had Tess decided to do this? Dumb, dumb, dumb. But now she had to say something. "I was wondering...I mean, where did you find that shirt?"

"It's in the back." The girl smiled. "They haven't brought

them out for display yet, but we got to look at them early."

Tess's heart sank. "Oh." She would have to come back again in a few days. If her mom could bring her, that was. If her mom wasn't in the hospital yet, having the baby.

"Are you a model?" Tess asked.

"No," the girl answered, grinning. "But I might be after today."

Braver now that the girl was friendly, Tess asked, "What do you mean?"

"Well, all of us here," she swept her hand out to indicate all the other models, "signed up for a modeling class through the community center. See that lady over there?" She pointed to a woman almost as tall as a flagpole with a thick roll of black hair.

Tess nodded.

The girl smiled. "She's the teacher, Miss Wakested. She used to be a professional model. We take classes for four days, and then we get to model here."

"Did you get to pick out your outfit?" Tess asked.

"Yep," the girl continued. "And we get to keep them, too. We buy them cheap. See that guy?" She pointed to the man wedged into the leather chair, flipping through pictures. "His name is Mr. Riggs. He's with a modeling agency. If he likes me and my picture, he'll talk to my parents, and then he might find some modeling jobs for me!"

"Wow," Tess said. *Maybe modeling school was just the thing she needed to help her look good.* "I wish I had known about this before."

"Well, you can still sign up. Miss Wakested is having one more class this summer, next week. I don't know if Mr. Riggs will be there for that class or not. So I don't know if you would have a chance to be a real model."

"Oh," Tess said.

"Do you want me to take you over to her?"

"Sure," Tess said, "if we can hurry." Even if Mr. Riggs might not be there next week, the outfit she liked would be.

The girl darted in and out through the crowd like a hummingbird, and Tess trailed her as best she could. Finally, they ended up next to Miss Wakested.

"This girl is interested in the class next week," Peachy Girl said.

Tess looked up. "Hi," she said. "Is it too late to sign up?"

"No," said Miss Wakested. "But you'll have to give me your name now."

"Well, I'm pretty sure I can come," Tess said. "I haven't asked my mom or anything, but I'm sure she'll say yes."

"The class starts on Monday at noon." Miss Wakested opened her notebook and took out a blue flier, showing directions to the class, describing what to wear and what the costs would be. "Here's all the information." After flipping a page in her day planner, she took out a pen. "If you want to sign up, I'll have to register your name now. But you need to be certain you'll be there. I won't be in the office again until class time on Monday."

Tess's heart jammed in high gear. "Okay," she answered. "I'll sign up, and so will my friend. My name is Tess Thomas, and my friend is Erin Janssen. We'll be there. For sure."

two

Modeling School

Saturday Afternoon, July 5

With the flier gripped in her shaking hand, Tess ran across the store to meet Erin.

"Did you find the shirt?" Erin had finished paying and was putting her receipt into her wallet.

"No. I mean, yes. I mean, kind of," Tess said as the two of them headed out of the store and into the mall. "The shirts are still in the back. They haven't brought them out yet. The model said they would be out next week."

"Well, then, we'll come back next week." Erin looked at her watch. "No time for a lemonade. There's a Coke machine by the door. We'll grab one of those instead. We're already thirty seconds late!"

"Run!" Tess said.

They made it to the mall exit and out the door. A blast of heat nearly knocked them back as they left the air-conditioned mall for the 100-degree Arizona heat. Tess glanced past some olive trees toward the street. Whew! She didn't see her mom's Jeep.

"Thank you, Lord!" she said, then turned toward Erin. "Go get us a Coke while I keep a lookout, okay?"

Erin nodded and hurried over to the machine and back. "Are you okay? You seem nervous. And what's in your hand?" Erin pointed to the paper Tess held.

"I'm not nervous, now that I see my mom's not here yet. I'm totally excited, that's what. It's something absolutely wonderful. An adventure!"

"Oh no, I feel trouble coming on," Erin said. "Just what kind of adventure?"

"Modeling school!" Tess said with a flourish. She sat down on a bench.

Erin sat beside her. "Okay, what did you do?"

Tess guzzled some of her Coke. Then she waved the paper Miss Wakested had given her. "Here, read this."

"'Modeling class for girls,'" Erin read. "'What is real beauty? We can help you find it—for keeps! Do you want social graces and etiquette? Sophistication, elegance, confidence, and great looks? Learn what colors work best on you, how to apply makeup to enhance your looks, and the proper way to walk, sit, and dine. Join us for the Scottsdale Community Center Modeling Class. The second and final session begins Monday, July 7.'"

Erin looked doubtful.

"You saw those girls today, didn't you?" Tess said. "They're not that different from us." She tried to ignore her own creeping doubt. "Are they?"

"I don't know," Erin said.

"Okay, okay," Tess said. "A couple of them looked a little more, well, glamorous. Elegant. But they've already been through the class. Maybe we'll look like that when we finish."

"*We* finish?"

"Oh, come on! Don't you want to?" Tess asked. "Even a little? You get to buy a new outfit—cheap—and after you model it, you keep it!"

Erin fanned the hot breeze toward herself with the flier, then read it over again. She slurped the last bit out of her can. "It might be fun. And it's not too expensive since it's at the community center. If our parents would let us."

Tess jumped up. "Of course they will! My mom was a model once. Just a few jobs, but she was even on a college calendar. If *she* can do it, I can, too. Don't you think?"

"Your mom is awfully pretty," Erin said.

Tess nodded slowly. That was true.

"But it *would* be fun," Erin continued. "Let's ask our parents. But speaking of your mom, I wish she would get here. It's hot out. Could we go wait inside?"

Tess frowned, a little squiggle of worry creeping up inside. "I don't know where she is. She made me promise not to be late. We can watch out the window."

Tess picked up her fanny pack, and just as the two of them began to walk indoors, a voice called out, "Erin! Tess!"

Tess turned around. *Erin's mom?* Her mom was supposed to pick them up, not Erin's mom. The girls walked toward Erin's family Suburban.

"Mom?" Erin called out. She frowned at Tess, her eyebrows all crinkled up.

"Get in, girls!" Erin's mom sang out.

"Does my mom know you're picking us up?" Tess asked.

"Your mom called me on the way to the doctor's office. She's had some contractions, and they're going to check it out."

A wave of fear rolled over Tess, washed back, and then rolled over her again. This might be it. The baby might be coming now. After all these months of waiting, was Tess ready?

"We'll just go back to my house and wait, okay?" Erin squeezed Tess's hand.

"Okay," Tess said. Soon after, they pulled into Erin's garage.

"Let's find you girls a snack," Erin's mother said. "And let me see what you bought."

Erin carried her shopping bag into the kitchen, and Tess followed. She looked around the kitchen. She liked Erin's mom, even though her kitchen was weird. Chicken decorations were everywhere. Chicks on the wallpaper, rooster and hen salt-and-pepper shakers, egg-shaped clock.

Erin's mom brought out a plastic tray of veggies and spicy-smelling dip.

"I'm not really hungry, thank you," Tess said. Her stomach was topsy-turvy. What if something was wrong with her mom or the baby?

"Erin, what a nice outfit you picked out!" Her mother admired the shorts and shirt.

Tom, Erin's older brother, came into the room and faked a girl's voice. "Oooh, Erin, you'll look so cute in that!"

"Get a life, will you?" Erin threw a baby carrot at Tom.

"Hi, Tess," Tom said. "Today might be the big day, huh?"

Tess smiled and blushed. "Maybe." Why did she always have to blush whenever Tom spoke to her? It would be nice if she could think of something clever to say in response. Instead, the dry spot was back in her throat.

"See ya!" Tom said, grabbing a handful of vegetables and heading out to the pool.

Erin munched on red pepper strips while her mother loaded the dishwasher.

"What did you buy today, Tess?" Mrs. Janssen asked.

"I couldn't find anything that looked good on me."

"But she did find out something exciting," Erin said. "And, uh, I hope you'll say yes to what we want to do."

Tess shifted uncomfortably. *Oh, great. Now if Erin's mother thinks modeling is dumb, she'll know it was my idea.*

"What's that?" Erin's mother asked.

"Well, some girls were in the junior department. And they were modeling clothes. We watched them for a while and saw some things we really liked. And you know how brave Tess is?" Erin smiled at her best friend. Tess smiled back.

"Well, she went up and talked to one of the models and was introduced to their teacher. A modeling class starts next week at the community center, and we want to go. Can we?"

Erin's mother wiped off her hands on a dishtowel. "I don't know." She reached for the paper Erin held out to her.

"Hmm. It looks like they teach ladylike walking and manners besides the modeling. And you do get a discount on an outfit, besides the low fee. I think it might be okay. We'll have to see what Tess's mom says though, with the baby and all."

"Oh yeah," Tess said. *What about the baby—and her mom? What was taking so long?*

"Let's go in my room," Erin said before biting into a cucumber slice.

"All right." Tess followed her down the hall.

Once there, Erin put in a CD, and Tess sat on the floor.

"I'm glad your mom said yes. Because I—well, I had to tell the teacher that we would be there."

"Tess! What if I didn't want to go?" Erin asked.

"Well, I guess I was hoping you would. I just knew it would be our only chance. I hope you're not mad that I promised for both of us."

Erin smiled. "I'm not mad. I hope your mom says yes though, or what will you do?" She sat on the floor, too. "I wonder if any of those girls will get modeling jobs."

Tess hit her forehead with her fist. "I can't believe I forgot to tell you!"

"What?" Erin sat cross-legged, rebraiding her loosened French braid.

Erin's bright orange kitty, Starlight, jumped up on Tess's lap, and Tess petted her silky fur. "Remember that man sitting in the big leather chair in the store?"

"No." Erin tied off the braid.

"He was looking at pictures while the girls walked? He kind of looked like a toad stuck in the chair?"

"Oh yeah."

"Well, he's from Miss Wakested's modeling agency. He was watching everyone there, and if he thought any of them would be good models, he was going to talk with their parents and maybe sign up the girls for other modeling jobs. If he comes back next week, maybe we could get jobs."

"Do you think we could?"

Tess shifted her position so her tummy didn't make that tiny roll over the waist of her shorts and so her legs looked longer. A lot of the girls modeling that day were really pretty. But modeling school would help, Tess knew it. "Why not?"

A sharp knock on the door interrupted the music.

Erin turned down the volume. "Yes?"

Her mother came into the room. "Tess's mom just called."

three

Pizza Pronto

Saturday Evening, July 5

Tess jumped up. "Is the baby coming? Is it here yet?"

"Yes, the baby's coming all right, just not yet," Erin's mom said. "Your mom was having false labor. That means she experienced signs that she might be having the baby, but she really wasn't."

Tess breathed a sigh of relief. "Great!"

"She called on her cell phone, and she'll be right over to pick you up. She's already picked up your brother and his friend." Erin's mother smiled and left the room.

"I was kind of worried," Tess said.

"I would be, too, if my mom was having a baby," Erin said.

"Oh," Tess said. "I just meant I was worried that if she was having the baby now we wouldn't be able to go to modeling school. Well, you might be able to, but I couldn't."

"I wouldn't do it without you!" Erin said. She jingled her Secret Sisters charm bracelet. "Remember our promise to do lots of things together this summer? Our Secret Sisters Plan?"

"Yeah," Tess agreed. "But to tell you the truth, I guess I'm a teensy bit worried about the other thing, too. Maybe more than a teensy bit, but I'm trying not to think about it."

"About your mom having a baby?"

"Yep." Tess took some lip gloss out of her fanny pack and slid it over her lips. Doing something normal made her feel less anxious.

"It's scary," Erin said. "I know people say bad things happen sometimes when you have a baby, and—"

Tess stopped putting on the lip gloss and looked at Erin, horrified.

Erin flushed. "I'm sorry. I'm really, really sorry. I shouldn't have said that. Nothing is going to happen to your mom. But maybe…do you want to pray about it?"

"Maybe later," Tess said, still shaken. "Let's think about modeling school and not about that for a while, okay?"

They walked down the long hallway toward Erin's front door. *Nothing bad is going to happen. Right, Lord?*

At the end of the hallway, they met Tom.

"I hear you two are going to modeling school. What for?"

"To learn how to train dogs." Erin made a face at Tom. "To model, of course. Why?"

"Why? I mean, it's not like you're going to be a model or anything."

Tess forced a smile. "We might get to do some modeling afterward." *Maybe after she had gone to the school he would see her as model material. Now, she knew, he saw her like everyone else did. Plain.*

Tom shrugged. "Whatever." He walked toward his room.

"Boys just don't understand," Erin said.

"I know. And now I have to spend the evening with my brother and Big Al. Talk about trouble with boys."

"And look, here they are," Erin said. Tess's mother pulled into the driveway. Erin opened the front door for Tess. "Call me tomorrow. We'll start to plan what we'll wear to the first class on Monday, okay?"

"Okay!" Tess climbed into the Jeep. She looked carefully at her mom. Her face was a little tired, but she seemed really, truly okay. Tess relaxed. "Hi, Mom." She kissed her on the cheek.

"Hi, sweetheart." Her mom put the car into reverse, but the gear stuck as she began to back out. *Aaahh!* Some loose rocks on the driveway went shooting through the air as her mom spun the tires.

Please, God, don't let anyone from Erin's family be watching right now! Tess prayed.

"I see you weren't kidnapped at the mall, old girl." Tyler, Tess's nearly nine-year-old brother, called out from the backseat.

Tess turned around and glared. He didn't need to give their mother any more worries right now. Or make her decide Tess couldn't go to the mall alone anymore.

"Of course not, Sherlock," she said. Her brother wanted to be a detective when he grew up, so he always talked in a fake Sherlock Holmes accent. "And why are we so lucky to have you with us?" she said to Big Al.

"I'm spending the night," Al said.

"And we're going to Pizza Pronto!" Tyler said.

"I hope that's okay," Tess's mother said. "Dad wanted to stay home and finish up some work, and I'm too tired to cook anything right now."

Usually that would be fine. But tonight Tess was hoping for some private time to talk with her mom about modeling. And she absolutely didn't want Big Al to hear.

She sighed. "It's okay." She felt inside her fanny pack to make sure the paper was still there. Better to talk with her mom alone about the classes. But the timing had to be perfect. Dad might not understand, being a man and all. But her mom would understand, having been a model before. At least Tess hoped she would.

Soon afterward Mrs. Thomas turned into the Pizza Pronto parking lot.

"Oh dear, I didn't see that." Tess's mom drove the car over the curb as she made the turn, almost crushing a purple prickly pear cactus. Tess closed her eyes and held her breath until her mom shut off the car's engine.

Tess looked back at Tyler, who was trying not to laugh, and Big Al, who was gripping his armrest for dear life.

"We're here!" Mrs. Thomas called out happily. "Everyone out."

After ordering and getting their drinks, they sat down. "Table, not a booth," Mrs. Thomas said. "I can't squeeze this big tummy into a booth anymore."

Tyler gulped down his Coke and turned to Big Al. "Let's deposit some funds into the animated entertainment center!"

"Huh?" Big Al said.

"Play video games, old chap!" Tyler said.

Big Al stood up, burping really loudly. Every person at every table around them turned to stare.

"Tess!" Big Al said, pointing an accusing finger at her. "Say 'Excuse me'!"

Tess turned raspberry red. "Cut it out!"

Laughing, Big Al and Tyler left the table for the video room.

"Mom, I just can't stand that kid. I really can't."

"Please, Tess, I'm too tired for this right now."

"Sorry." Tess noticed lines on her mother's face. "So tell me what happened at the hospital today. I was worried."

"I'm sorry you were worried, honey," her mother said, reaching an arm around her. "I was having some contractions last night and this morning, but then they didn't go away, so I went to get them checked out."

"But the baby's not coming?"

"Not quite yet, but soon. My body's warming up before the baby really comes. It could be anytime now. I'm already a little late."

Tess looked around. No pizza yet. No boys. She might as well bring up the modeling school idea.

"Read this!" Tess reached into her fanny pack and took out the modeling-school paper.

Her mom read over the paper. Tess watched her face, looking for a smile, a frown, anything. But nothing crossed her mom's face.

"It looks interesting," she finally said.

Uh-oh.

"We saw some of the girls doing their modeling assignment today at the mall. It looked really cool and fun, and a lot of great things could happen like new clothes and modeling afterward. Erin and I really want to sign up." The words tumbled out like a waterfall. "Is that okay?"

Tess left off the part about how she already had told Miss Wakested they would be there Monday.

Her mother leaned back in her chair, the tired lines on her face deeper than they'd been a few minutes before.

She looked as if she was going to say something, then the waiter brought their steaming pizza to the table. He rolled the sharp slicer through the crust, cutting the pizza into pieces before leaving.

Quick! Say something before the boys come back to eat! Tess thought.

"I'm sorry, Tess. Not this time."

four

Hopes and Dreams

Saturday Night, July 5

"But—" Tess started.

Big Al and Tyler ran up. "Food!"

She wasn't going to say anything now. She definitely didn't want to talk about her mom's decision with Big Al and Tyler at the table, so she picked at the cheese while the others ate. Then they went home.

"I'm going to my room, okay?" Tess said as they walked into the house.

"Okay," her mother said. Tyler and Big Al didn't bother to answer.

Once in her room, Tess flicked on the light switch, which also turned on the CD player. An "El Shaddai Remix" started to play. After a few minutes of soothing music, she logged on to her computer diary.

> *Dear Lord,*
>
> *I'm not feeling good at all. In fact, I'm feeling very bad. I'm not sure I'm ready for the baby. And what if something happens to my mom when the baby*

comes? Or what if something is wrong with the baby and it dies?

I feel selfish even bringing this up, but I really want to go to modeling school. I'm a plain-vanilla-looking girl, and I want to be strawberry supreme. Special. Jazzy. And besides, I already told Miss Wakested that we would be there. What should I do, God? Tell me, please.

Love, You-Know-Who

Tess sat down on her floor and began to paint her toenails. Her mom's toenails were always painted. In fact, her mom always looked pretty. If Tess could learn a few things at modeling school, then, maybe...

A sudden thought came to her. *Maybe it was the driving. Yeah, that's it! What if Erin's mom would do all the driving? There's no swim team this coming week since the instructors have competition. So Mom won't have to do anything at all!*

Tess capped the polish and fanned some air over her toes. "Come on, hurry up and dry!" she shouted at her feet. Her dad would kill her if she tried walking now and got polish on the carpet.

As soon as the purple toe tips were ready, she raced into the family room where her mom was watching TV. Tess almost spoke, but when she looked at her mother's face, she stopped. Her mom looked so hot and tired. She didn't need any more stress.

"Did you want something, Tess?" her mother asked.

Tess's shoulders slumped. "Uh, no. I mean, forget it. It's okay."

Her mom smiled wearily and patted the couch next to her. "Come and sit down, okay?"

Tess snuggled next to her. As she leaned against her mother, she felt her mom's tummy tightening.

"What was that?" Tess said with alarm.

"Just a contraction. Not long now, is it?"

"I guess not." Tess looked down. When there were three kids, instead of two, she would be less important.

"Things will be different when the baby is here, won't they? I'll be busier for a while, and it won't be quiet, and it'll be hard for me to do the things I've always done for you. At least for a few months."

"I guess so," Tess said. She was quiet for a minute before asking, "What if it's a girl?"

"Then you'll have a sister. Wouldn't that be neat?"

Tess looked down. "What will that make me?"

"A big sister, of course."

Tess said nothing.

Her mother pulled her closer. "You'll always be special to me, Tess. You'll always be my firstborn child. When Tyler was born, I still loved you just as much. When this baby is born, we'll all have someone else to love. But it won't change my love for you. Nothing could." She chuckled. "Not even your best homemade fried chicken."

"Mom!" Tess hit her mom's shoulder playfully. Leave it to her mother to remind her of the time Tess set the house on fire trying to make her mom's favorite fried chicken.

"Tell me about modeling class."

Tess perked up. "Well, they learn lots of things, like that flier said. And I'm going to be in junior high, soon, you know. I want to be special, look good. I need help. I think modeling school can do that, don't you?"

"You look special already," her mom answered.

"You had a chance to be a model. Can't I?" Tess begged.

Her mother nodded slowly. "Maybe I said no too quickly. If this is something you really want, and Erin's mother will drive if the baby comes, you can sign up."

Tess pulled away from her mom and jumped off the couch. "Are you kidding? That's great!"

"I'm not kidding," her mother said. "But you'll have to pay the class fee out of your baby-sitting money. I'll buy the outfit, as long as you choose something you can wear to school in September. Okay?"

"Okay! I'm going to call Erin right now." She skidded halfway out of the room then turned around and ran back to her mother. She threw her arms around her mom and squeezed her shoulders before giving her a big smooch on the cheek. "I love you."

Tess looked at her mom's face, every bit as beautiful when she was tired as when she was not. "Mom?"

"Yes, Tess?"

"What if something's wrong with the baby? Or goes wrong with you?"

"Most likely nothing will happen," her mom said. "Don't worry."

five

Talent Scouting!

Monday, July 7

Tess paced back and forth in front of the door. Modeling school was only a few minutes away. Her life would change. She would look better and get a few modeling jobs.

"If you don't stop that, you're going to get your outfit sweaty," her mother said.

"Oh no!" Tess lifted her arm to check. No sweat. Good thing she had tried her new deodorant this morning. Still, she had better stop pacing.

"I'll be there to pick you up when class is over," her mother added.

"Okay, Mom." Tess pecked her mom on the cheek as Erin's mother drove into the driveway.

"Do you have the check?"

Tess nodded.

"Have a good time!" Her mother opened the door, and Tess scooted out and into the waiting car.

"Oh, you look great," Erin said as Tess shut the car door. Erin's mother backed out into the street.

"Today, Tess is wearing a cap-sleeved dress in a multicolored floral print with a solid lining. On her neck is a floral link choker," Tess imitated the modeling announcer they had heard last week and flipped back her hair.

Erin giggled. "And Erin is wearing a purple botanical skirt with an all-over floral print. In her hair are Little Dipper star clips. Aren't these girls lovely, folks? Let's give them a round of applause."

Erin's mother laughed. "You two! I think you'll have a great time."

"Why do you think they had us bring coats?" Erin asked. She held up a floor-length raincoat. "I mean, it's one hundred degrees out!"

"I don't know," Tess said.

Erin's mother pulled into the Scottsdale Community Center's parking lot. "I guess you'll find out soon!"

Erin and Tess hopped out of the Suburban. "Tess's mother will be here in a few hours. See you soon!" Mrs. Janssen said.

The girls waved, and Erin's mom drove off.

Several other girls made their way into the classroom. It was a big, deep cave of a room with high ceilings and bright lights. The center table was really a long runway, shaped like a giant *T*, in the middle of the room, with chairs set all around it. Cold shots of air conditioning froze the room.

"Maybe that's why we had to bring coats!" Erin whispered as they hung their coats on the coat rack with the others. "Do you want to sit here?" she asked, pointing to two open seats. Tess noticed a girl sitting all alone at the far end.

"Let's sit down by that girl," Tess said. "She looks lonely."

Erin nodded, and the two of them sat down, with Tess between Erin and the new girl.

The girl turned toward Tess, and Tess got a good look at her face for the first time. Her warm violet eyes were framed with thick lashes.

She's gorgeous, Tess thought. "Hi! My name is Tess."

"My name is Lila."

"I'm Erin."

The three girls nodded but didn't say much. They didn't need to because Miss Wakested came into the room. Her tall, thin shadow cast a line down the center of the runway.

"Take a seat, girls," she said, clapping her hands lightly. "I've placed an outline of our class in front of each seat." Miss Wakested stopped talking and stared disapprovingly out at the girls. Some of them leaned on the table, others sat cross-legged in their chairs or with the chair legs leaning back.

"Today we'll learn the proper way to sit."

Tess unwrapped her legs from the chair legs and put them in front of her, under the table.

"Next we'll learn how to stand properly and how to walk on a catwalk." Miss Wakested motioned to the runway in the center. "And we'll practice the correct way to go down stairs. Finally, we'll learn how to put on and take off our coats like young ladies."

"I think I already know how to put on a coat," Tess whispered to Erin. She was going to say the same thing to Lila. But Lila looked upset, her hands balled up.

"Are you okay?" Tess whispered to her.

"I didn't know we were supposed to bring a coat," Lila whispered back. "I don't have one!"

"You can borrow mine," Tess reassured her.

Erin poked Tess. She blushed as she realized Miss Wakested was staring at her. Tess pressed her lips together. No more whispering.

"Finally, a friend of mine might stop by for a visit," Miss Wakested said. "One I'm certain you'll enjoy meeting."

Tess and Erin exchanged glances. Miss Wakested must mean the modeling agent!

For almost an hour the girls took turns learning how to sit with their legs crossed discreetly at the ankles, then to stand and walk with their shoulders back and chin up. They practiced: legs down, legs crossed, arms folded in front of them, arms open at their sides. It was tiring, and none of this was going to help Tess look good in school.

"I feel like Pinocchio!" Erin said. She jerked her arms and legs into the air and flailed them about.

"Miss Janssen, are you having some kind of problem?" Miss Wakested called from the other side of the room.

Erin turned lava red hot. "No, uh, I'm fine, thanks."

Miss Wakested smiled, her first touch of softness. "Then perhaps you're ready to walk down the stairs. Please come forward."

Oh, Lord, don't let Erin do something embarrassing, Tess prayed. *Me either, when it's my turn,* she added.

She needn't have worried. Erin walked down the steps at an angle, like a proper lady, without a problem.

Next, Tess. One step after another, softly, copying what Miss Wakested had shown them Whew! No stumbles.

After Tess went, Lila did. She practically floated.

"She must have practiced," Tess whispered to Erin, forgetting her promise to herself to keep her lips pursed closed.

As Lila walked back to her seat, the toadlike man entered the room.

"Erin!" Tess squeezed her friend's hand under the table. "That's him."

Erin opened her eyes wide but glanced at Miss Wakested and said nothing.

All chatter stopped. Tess could hear her watch ticking.

Miss Wakested went to greet her guest. All eyes were riveted on the two of them.

"Girls, remember my telling you we might have a very special guest? I'd like to introduce my friend and former agent, Mr. Riggs."

Mr. Riggs smiled from the doorway, where his body took up the whole frame.

A wisp of hair escaped Miss Wakested's clip, and she quickly tucked it behind her ear. "I don't model professionally anymore, but when I did, Mr. Riggs was my agent. He works out of Los Angeles but is here to shoot several local commercials. While he's in the area, he'll also be talent scouting."

Tess squeezed Erin's hand under the table again, and Erin squeezed back. Tess glanced over at Lila, who was staring at Mr. Riggs.

"He'll review your professional portraits, which will be taken on Thursday. And Friday, he'll be at Robinson's-May to watch you model."

All right! They would have their chance after all! A buzz of excitement rose from the room.

Miss Wakested put her finger to her lips, and everyone hushed.

"All of you are lovely young ladies. If Mr. Riggs thinks any of you have professional potential, he'll meet with you and your parents to discuss the possibilities." She turned toward Mr. Riggs. "Do you have anything to say, Jason?"

"I'm delighted to consider the talent among your students. I'm hoping to find several girls with the look I want. Work hard, and it might be you!"

Miss Wakested smiled. "The class will be over in thirty minutes," she said to him. "We can talk more then."

Mr. Riggs waved a friendly hand and left the room.

Just a few more days to look good. Tess pushed away her doubts. *Surely the makeup session will help. I'll work hard, like he said.*

"Did you hear that?" Erin breathed out as quietly as she could. "He's looking for models!"

Tess said nothing but squeezed Erin's hand again, this time harder than ever.

six

The Calendar

Monday Evening, July 7

Tess was flying high after class, planning how she could look her best by Thursday, absolutely by Friday. But a faint signal of trouble reached her, the one she usually sensed when her dad disapproved. He said nothing about modeling all through dinner.

Tess cleared the table and brought the topic up herself. "Dad, modeling school was so cool. I mean, some of it was a little boring. Like learning to take off your coat. But tomorrow we're going to learn what colors look best on us. That will be really fun. And then I'll know what clothes to buy to look great at school this year." She watched his face.

"You always look great, cupcake." But he smiled as he poured some detergent into the dishwasher and turned it on.

Tess exhaled, relieved.

"I'm going to do a little paperwork. I want to be caught up, just in case." He looked at Tess's mother.

Mrs. Thomas stood up. "I still haven't cleared out the

closet in the baby's room. I wanted to finish my last ad piece first. But now that's in the mail, so I better finish the closet. I have to get rid of some board games and leftover toys from kids' meals and move the boxes of pictures."

"Boxes of pictures?" Tess asked. The old college calendar! She remembered seeing it last year, but was it still there? "I could help you clean it out."

"That's really kind of you, honey. Thanks."

"Don't lift anything heavy!" her dad said to her mother as he left the room. "Call me."

As Tess and her mom walked into the room, Tess flipped on the light switch. The room glowed softly. Her mom had put dim light bulbs into the sockets so the room wouldn't be too bright.

"How about if I sit in the closet and push everything out so you can reach it better?" Tess asked.

"Good idea." Her mother plopped down in the rocking chair. "Want to feel some major kicking?"

Tess put her hand over her mother's belly. Pow!

"Man, that kid is strong!"

"A football player, maybe, or a ballerina." Her mother smiled. "Let's get busy. We both have a big day tomorrow."

After settling in the closet, Tess still couldn't see the picture box. It had to be there. She would just have to clear some other junk out of the way first. "Should we save this?" She held up Candy Land. "I mean, Tyler and I don't play it anymore."

"But we might want to in a few years," her mother reminded her. "When the little kicker gets bigger."

"Oh yeah." Tess set it to the "save" side. She tossed handfuls of discarded little toys and broken crayons into the trash. "What about this?" She held up some faded Christmas wrapping paper.

"Garbage," her mother said.

Bingo! Tess saw what she was looking for and pulled it out front.

"Let's look at some of these, okay?" She picked up a handful of photos from the picture box.

"I really should put those pictures in albums," her mother said. "They're all just tossed in there."

"Oh, Mom, look! A picture of Tyler when he was a baby." Tess giggled. "He's got spaghetti in his hair and up his nose. Gross!" She passed the picture over to her mother.

Her mom laughed. "To think this is the same kid who now washes his sneakers."

"Can I keep this picture out?"

"What are you going to do with it?"

"Show it to Big Al." Tess set it aside. "They always make fun of me."

"Look, Tess," her mother said. "There's one of your baby pictures."

Tess grabbed it. She was standing in front of her grandma's house picking a flower. She must have been about eighteen months old. *And even then I had chubby legs,* she thought, staring at the rubber rolls on her thighs just below the pink ruffle of her baby bloomers.

"Oh, you were so darling. I'll never forget taking that picture. You were the apple of everyone's eye. The first grandchild."

"Do you really remember me when I was a baby?" Tess asked.

"Of course," her mother said.

Tess pulled out a picture of the four of them posing for a professional family portrait last summer. "I guess we'll have to get a new portrait done, right?"

"Right," her mother said. Quietly, Tess set that picture on the "save" pile, too. Maybe she would put it on her bulletin board.

Where was that calendar? She dug through the box. *I know it was in here. Maybe it got lost.*

She reached down into the box where she couldn't see and felt for the calendar. She grabbed hold of it. "Aha!"

"Aha, what?"

"This!" Tess pulled out the yellowed, ragged-edged calendar with a flourish.

Her mother laughed. "I'd forgotten how fascinated you were with that. Is that why you agreed to help me clean out this closet?"

Tess blushed. "Well, when you said picture box, it reminded me that I wanted to see this. But I wanted to help you anyway."

Tess turned the calendar's pages. Past January. Past February and March. April.

"Here you are." Tess stared at a picture of her much younger mother.

"Yes, there I am." Her mom smiled.

On the April page of the campus calendar, Tess's mom stood in front of her college's journalism department. Two large cacti flanked her, and a little cactus at her feet bloomed snowball white blossoms. The Arizona sky, as always, was a clear liquid blue. Her mom's confident smile beamed out from the page. She wore jeans, a light summer sweater, and a straw hat. In her hand was a journalist's notebook.

"Did you like being a model?" Tess asked.

"It was okay."

"How did you start?"

Her mom leaned back in the rocking chair and closed her eyes, remembering while she talked.

"One of my professors was in charge of the calendar, and she asked me if I'd like to pose. It paid a little, and I said yes. That led to a few more jobs while I was in school."

"Did you love it? Was it awesome?"

"It was okay. Sometimes I had a really good time. But sometimes I got tired of having people pull at my clothes and tug my hair."

Tess hugged the calendar close to her chest and closed her eyes, too. If she were modeling for real, she would never get tired of it. She would know for sure she looked special. Maybe her picture would end up in a calendar or something, just like her mom's. Tess could model job after job and love it forever.

seven ✳

Autumn and Spring

Tuesday, July 8

Tess paced the hallway. It was almost time for class to
begin.

"Come on, Tyler, I don't want to be late!" Tess called out.
"The lizard can wait."

Why does he have to feed Hercules right now? "My class
starts in fifteen minutes, and we still have to pick up Erin."
She could imagine Miss Wakested marking a little black
X by Tess's name and frowning as Tess walked into the
classroom. Late. Not at all like a professional model.

She remembered Miss Wakested's warm smile yester-
day. *Well, maybe she's like an orange, tough on the outside
but sweet on the inside.*

"I say, old girl, I'm coming." Tyler hustled down the hall.
"He's not a lizard. He's a horned toad. I just have to wash
these leftover cricket legs off my hands." He ran them
under the kitchen sink and then rushed out to the Jeep.

Tess rushed out, too, and beeped the car's horn. Her
mom came into the garage looking none too happy.

"Don't honk at me, young lady," she said, struggling to fasten the seat belt underneath her big belly.

"Sorry, Mom," Tess said. "Here, I'll open the garage door for you."

Her mom roared out of the garage and down the street toward Erin's.

"I say, why are you having a panic attack about Mr. Big Rig?" Tyler said.

"His name is Mr. Riggs, and I'm not worried about that. I just like to be on time, that's all," Tess said.

But she smiled. Mr. Big Rig. He did kind of look like a truck.

"Since when are you so on-time?" Tyler asked.

"All right, you two," their mother intervened. "I'm not feeling well right now, so let's not fight."

Tess and Tyler looked at one another.

"I guess we'd better cool off, old fruit. Don't want to start anything," Tyler whispered, jerking his thumb at their mother, "if you know what I mean."

A few minutes later Tess and Erin walked into the community center's big cave of a room just as Miss Wakested began to talk. They slipped into their seats next to Lila.

"All right, ladies, today we're going to work on our colors. As I'm sure some of you have noticed, certain colors look better on you than others. We'll discover a whole palette of colors that bring out the best in you. From these you will choose your clothing, your makeup, even your accessories so that you are simply stunning! Please find a partner to work with you."

Tess and Erin turned toward one another. Out of the corner of her eye, Tess noticed Lila. No one came near her.

"Clarice, would you please partner with Lila?" Miss Wakested said.

Clarice rolled her eyes and lugged her notebook over to where Lila sat. "I wanted to stay with my friends!"

Lila stiffened.

Miss Wakested set out several huge boxes of scarves.

"A very smart woman figured out that each of us corresponds to a season: either winter, spring, summer, or autumn. Our hair color, eye color, and skin color all work together to look good with some tones and poor with others. First, take the quiz in your notebook to try to determine what season you might be. Then hold up some scarves and look in the mirror to pinpoint which colors work best for you. Your partner can help."

Miss Wakested continued, "Afterward, pick up one of these sheets for your season. You can take it shopping with you to help you make the best selections." She set a stack of papers on the table.

After they did their quizzes, Tess grabbed a bunch of scarves and took them back to where she and Erin sat. On her way back, she noticed that Clarice was looking in the mirror but ignoring Lila.

"Let me start with you, okay?" Erin asked.

"You're the artist," Tess agreed and faced her friend. After holding up several scarves in front of Tess and checking the quiz questions, they decided she was an autumn.

"Look, I'm a gypsy!" Tess held up an orange-red scarf in front of her face.

"All right, gypsy, help me figure out my colors." Erin turned out to be a spring.

They each snagged a color chart for their season. Now when they went shopping, they would buy the best colors.

"Look out, junior high, here come Tess Autumn and Erin Spring!" Erin joked.

Tess smiled. But on her way back to her seat, she looked over at Lila.

Clarice held up some awful colors for Lila. Clarice was acting crazy, trying to get her friends at the other end of the table to laugh and pay attention to her since she was separated from them against her will. "There. That looks good." She laughed, but it was a mean laugh, empty of joy.

"Do you think so?" Lila looked in the mirror, and Tess saw the disbelief on Lila's face.

"She's not helping Lila. She's picking ugly colors!" Tess told Erin, then Tess went over to stand behind Lila. "Can I help, too?" she asked. "Erin and I finished early."

"Yes, please!" Lila said.

Clarice looked embarrassed. "We're only supposed to be with our partners. So butt out."

Tess sat down next to Lila anyway. Erin sat firmly behind her.

"I'd like them to help," Lila said quietly.

"Fine. I didn't want to be your partner anyway." Clarice grabbed her color chart, on which Lila had made neat marks, and ran back to the other end of the table.

Lila frowned.

"Don't worry," Erin said. "She's just jealous. And probably mad because she wasn't with her friends."

Miss Wakested walked over. "Is everything all right? Where's Clarice?"

"It's okay," Lila said. "I'm mostly done, and Clarice went back to her seat."

Tess brought over a new handful of scarves, and she and Erin helped Lila figure out she was a summer. Even though, actually, she looked great in almost every season except the one Clarice had chosen.

After class, Erin's mom picked up Tess and Erin. They sat way in the back of the Suburban where they had some privacy to plan their shopping trip.

"My colors are kind of, well, weird," Tess said. "I mean, mustard? Brown? Olive? I wish I was a spring, like you."

"Peach is on there." Erin pointed to Tess's chart. "Like that shirt at the mall."

"I still wish I looked like you," Tess said. "You're much prettier."

"No way!" Erin said. "If I had my hair cut short, I'd look like a boy. At least you have a nice figure."

"Oh yeah. I jiggle like pudding with a skin on it when I walk."

Erin laughed. "No, you don't!"

I'm not kidding. "Well, my legs do," Tess said.

"Nobody's perfect," Erin said.

Tess bit her nail. "I know someone who is."

"Lila," Erin said.

"Yeah." Tess gathered up her stuff. "I like her a lot, but I sort of hope she doesn't model before or after me at Robinson's-May on Friday."

eight

Dining Out Darlings

Wednesday, July 9

The next day at class a fancy luncheon was planned for the students to practice their manners. But first, they had a session about makeup.

Have to look great tomorrow for pictures. Work hard and all that, Tess reminded herself.

"Pay attention, girls." Miss Wakested clapped her hands lightly. "We have only a short time to go over skin care and makeup basics because the van will be here soon to take us to our luncheon."

Tess stared in the lighted mirror in front of her. She flipped the mirror over to the magnification side. "Whoa, scary!"

"What?" Erin asked. She plucked one eyebrow while looking into her mirror.

"My pores. When you look at them on this side of the mirror, they look like craters."

Erin smiled. "At least you have nice eyebrows. Mine go so far back I look like an alien. Do you think Mr. Riggs will hire an alien?"

Tess giggled.

"Now," Miss Wakested started, "the first basic is keeping clean skin. Many of you are concerned with pimples and breakouts, I know. The first step to prevention is clean skin. Clip back your hair, please."

"Speaking of pimples," Tess whispered, "I was hoping to keep my hair over my forehead since I think I'm getting one." But she clipped back her hair anyway.

Miss Wakested showed them how to use a soft cloth and some cleansing lotion to keep their skin clean, followed by a cotton ball dipped in ice blue astringent.

Tess rubbed it over her skin, and it tingled.

"I think that pimple is drying up right now," she whispered to Erin. "I feel it working!"

Erin rolled her eyes and capped her minibottle of astringent.

"Next comes some light moisturizer. This moisturizer, specially formulated for preteens and teenagers, provides a base for your makeup, so don't skip it," Miss Wakested said. "It won't cause oily skin."

Tess smoothed some over her cheeks. It smelled like rose water and made her skin silky.

"Now I'm going to hand out some compacts with testers of makeup. Lila, will you please help me pass these out?"

Lila stood up and took the box from Miss Wakested.

"Lila is sitting by Josie today," Erin whispered.

"Good!" Tess turned to look at Josie, with her smooth black hair and walnut skin. Another gorgeous bombshell. Tess felt her hopes start to sink slowly.

"I'm glad Lila's found somebody," Erin said, smiling. "Like I have you!"

"You know it." Tess smiled at Lila as she handed her a makeup set, and Lila grinned back.

"Now, girls," Miss Wakested said, "young ladies don't need much makeup—unless you're on a professional modeling shoot. If that comes about, you'll have a makeup artist to help you."

She opened one of the compacts. "Remember, you have the beauty of youth. More often than not, makeup covers up your natural beauty and hides it behind something artificial. I'm sure most of you have seen people with too much makeup on."

Tess and Erin nodded. Lauren, from the popular crowd in their school, had started to wear way too much makeup. Frosted eye shadow and everything.

"I don't like foundation for girls, which turns the skin orange or leaves a line on the chin that says 'Makeup stopped here!' And your skin is so beautiful you don't need powder. Instead, use a little light blush just on your cheekbone, like so." Miss Wakested demonstrated. "Please open your compacts and apply a light brush stroke or two."

Tess and Erin complied and then followed Miss Wakested's instruction for lip gloss.

"Again, young ladies don't need color, just shine. If you must use a little color, please use something light that's blended into the gloss."

"Remember our first day as friends?" Tess asked. "We told each other what kind of lip gloss we used?"

Erin nodded. "Want to pick a new kind to change flavors as we go into junior high?"

"Okay," Tess said. "Let's buy some at the drugstore when we go to pick out the rest of the makeup for Friday."

After a light coat of beige eye shadow and a slick of mascara, the girls looked at one another.

"You're gorgeous!" Erin said.

Tess blushed. "Not as gorgeous as you!"

Shortly after the makeup session, they boarded the van that took them to their luncheon. With all her makeup on, Tess felt as if she deserved to dine in such a fancy place. She finally was growing up.

When they walked into the room set aside especially for them, Tess drew in her breath. "I haven't been somewhere this fancy since my mom took me to lunch at the beginning of last year!"

They pulled out plush chairs and sat down. Like a queen, Miss Wakested ruled at the head of the long table. Rows and rows of silverware and four plates were set at each place, along with two crystal goblets, a large one for water and a narrow one for milk. Each girl had a tiny bud vase containing a pink rose in front of her place at the table.

"Definitely worth the ten extra bucks for lunch!" Tess whispered. "Just don't make me giggle like a little girl."

Erin made a clown face, and Tess turned away, smiling.

Over the courses of salad and rolls, petite steaks, and chocolate torte, Miss Wakested taught them which forks to use, how to hold a knife, which glasses to use, and how to carry on a conversation with grace. Tess spoke quietly to both Erin and the girls across the table from her.

"No pinkies up when you're holding a glass!" Miss Wakested warned, then smiled.

Erin's mother was waiting for them outside the restaurant after lunch.

"Oh no, my brothers came," Erin said as she looked into the Suburban's windows.

Tess's tummy tumbled. Tom was in the car.

"Hi, girls, did you have a good time?" Erin's mother asked.

"Yes, it was awesome!" Erin said. "And tomorrow is picture day with the professional photographer!"

They buckled up, and Erin's mother took off.

"I'm kind of nervous," Tess admitted, "because Mr. Riggs is going to use those pictures on Friday when he makes his decision."

"You look nice," Tom said. "No matter what Mr. Riggs says."

"Thanks." Remembering her ladylike manners over lunch, Tess smiled quietly. But she beamed on the inside all the way to her house.

nine

Picture Perfect

Thursday Afternoon, July 10

Tess tucked her hair back into barrettes. "Does it look all right?" She smoothed the front of her gold-colored shirt. "I spent a lot of time picking out the best colors. I thought of olive because I have an olive shirt, but it had long sleeves. And I don't want to be sweaty."

"Tess, you look fantastic!" Erin assured her.

The photographer from Picture Perfect Photography worked to set up his camera at the end of the runway inside their classroom.

"You look great, too. I mean, really. I'm so glad we did our colors because now we know what looks best."

"You're chattering, goofy!" Erin said.

"I know. I'm so excited! Remind me to bring my color chart when we go shopping tonight. I want to make sure I buy something good. Maybe the peach shirt. But maybe not, since Mr. Riggs already saw it."

"I know, but you should buy what you really want," Erin said.

"I will, don't worry. My mom said she would come by right after dinner to pick you up. She wants to go to the mall with us since she might not get to take me out for a while after the baby comes. Okay?"

"Of course," Erin said.

"First up, Josie!" the photographer said, consulting his list.

Josie was a natural, her black hair twisted in a gold clip, her skin perfect. The photographer took at least fifteen shots of her. It didn't take long at all. So many pictures!

"Tess, you're next."

"Go, girl!" Erin squeezed Tess's cold hand.

Why did she have to be second? Watching others might have given her some time to soothe her nerves.

"Have a seat," the photographer said.

Tess perched on a stool while he adjusted the lighting.

"Which way should I look?" she asked, smiling.

"Right at the lens," the photographer said. He talked to her but never really looked at her.

"Okay, honey, smile for me!" he finally said.

He snapped two shots of her face, one of the front and one of her profile, then asked her to walk down the runway.

"Now?" Tess asked. He had taken at least five shots of Josie's face. Maybe he had lost count.

"Now!" he snapped. "We have a lot of other pictures to take here, so move along."

Shaken, Tess moved to the back of the runway and then walked toward him while he snapped a few pictures. *Don't let me cry. Even though my heart is cracked into twenty pieces, don't let it show on my face, Lord. I don't want to mess up these pictures.*

At the end, he asked her last name, wrote it in the note-book near the camera, and thanked her. She walked back to her seat.

I'm just not pretty enough. I'll never be strawberry supreme or anything other than plain vanilla. Boring. Average.

"What's the matter?" Erin said, looking at Tess's face.

"Didn't you see what happened?"

"What? You did great! The lighting was just right on you."

"But he only took two pictures of my face and three or four while I was walking."

"So?" Erin said.

Tess sipped out of her water bottle. It calmed her. She definitely didn't want to lose it in front of everyone. "He took way more pictures of Josie."

"Maybe he was just getting his film ready with Josie," Erin said. "Since she was first."

Yes, that must be it. Tess sipped some more water. It tasted plain. Average.

She kept her head low, quieting her heart, while two or three other girls were photographed.

"Erin Janssen," Miss Wakested called, "you're next."

Tess squeezed Erin's hand.

Erin walked up to the chair while Tess watched. *Help her take some good pictures, Lord,* she prayed. But when she counted the photographer taking four pictures of Erin's face and at least six of her on the runway, Tess's heart fell like a stone dropped from a bridge.

It wasn't a problem with the film after all. It's something wrong with me. I've always known it. And now everyone else does, too.

Erin stopped to talk with Miss Wakested afterward, and

Tess watched another girl go. Two face pictures. Three runway pictures. Just like he had done with Tess, and the other unremarkable girls.

Tess's stomach knotted tight when it was Lila's turn.

The Picture Perfect man snapped what seemed like dozens of pictures of Lila's face, at least as many as Josie's. And Tess couldn't keep up with the flashing lights that told how many snapshots he took of Lila as she walked down the catwalk.

Lila smiled at Tess as she went back to her seat near Josie. Tess forced a smile back. It wasn't Lila's fault.

Anger brewed within her. But it was someone's fault. *I used my baby-sitting money for this, and I paid just as much as everyone else. I should get the same number of pictures. This is totally unfair! It's not unfair, it's reality. I'm not even average. I'm below average. Ugly.*

Tess closed her eyes and tried to decide if she should say anything.

"Tess?" Erin said.

Tess shook her head no and turned away. She didn't want to talk to Erin right now.

I'm going to say something to Miss Wakested. She considered a lot of possibilities. But as she did, she recalled a Bible verse. "Always be humble and gentle."

I'm humble, Lord. This is so totally humbling. And not by my choice. She couldn't think of anything gentle to say. So she said nothing at all.

Her mom had yet another doctor's appointment, so Tess's dad, who had left work early, picked up Tess and Erin at the community center. After dropping off Erin, they drove home.

"You're pretty quiet. How did the pictures go?" her dad asked as they pulled into the driveway.

"Okay."

"Just okay? You were so excited this morning."

"Just okay," Tess said in a voice that meant "Don't ask any more."

Dad said nothing except, "Will you please get the mail? I'm going inside to do a little work till your mother comes home."

"All right." Tess dragged herself to the mailbox and then inside the house. At least she had received some mail. She flipped open the magazine Grandma Kate had given her a subscription to last year. Page after page of pictures of perfect girls with perfect bodies in perfect clothes with perfect skin.

"Picture perfect," Tess said, her voice prickly. *I guess I'm supposed to be gentle even when I'm talking to myself.*

Wandering into the family room, she turned on the television. Soap operas and commercials. Perfect people again, except for the man talking about heartburn medicine, and he didn't count.

"Why can't normal people be on TV?" she shouted, clicking it off.

She heard Tyler playing Game Boy in his room.

Guess I'll go lie on my bed.

On her way to her room, she passed her mom and dad's room. Her mother's closet door was open. *Mom won't care if I try on a few things. Maybe all I need is some new clothes.* Tess tiptoed in and scooped out a few outfits.

Please, God, let something help me look better. Anything! She ran out of the room and into the bathroom, clicking the door shut.

She put on one of her mom's shirts. "I always liked this one. It's tomato red. That's one of my colors."

She twisted her hair up like Josie had worn hers, but every time Tess tried to put in the clip, it fell out. Then she tried braiding her hair. She looked like a prairie girl. She finally settled on that morning's barrettes.

She snapped her fingers. "Makeup!" She unlocked the bathroom door and ran into the kitchen to get her fanny pack with the makeup compact that Miss Wakested had given each girl. "I didn't do it right, didn't put enough on today. That was the problem!"

Back into the bathroom.

"Maybe a little more blush, right here." She swiped the brush over her cheekbones again and again.

"Oh no!" Bright reddish spots was not the look she was hoping for. "Circus Clown Central. Try again."

She scrubbed off the blush with the cleansing foam. Then she applied the blue astringent and some rose-water moisturizer.

This time the blush went on okay, but a wisp of hair fell out of the barrette again. And the pimple was actually growing bigger.

"I'm not giving up!" She stroked some mascara on her lashes.

The powder from the blush must have tickled her nose because she sneezed. And as she did, she closed her eyes. When she opened them again, spidery black lines fanned out under her eyes. The mascara hadn't dried yet.

Nothing was going to help. Nothing could help.

"Help!" She dabbed some astringent on a cotton ball to wipe off the smeared mascara, but the bottle spilled and splashed onto her mom's tomato red shirt.

It was all too much. Ripping the clips out of her hair, Tess scrubbed the makeup off with what was left of the moisturizer sample. Then she leaned in close to the mirror and stuck out her tongue at herself. Hot tears slipped down her cheeks, smearing the mascara even worse.

"Why try?" she said. "Nothing is going to change the fact that I am an ugly frog!"

As she pulled away from the mirror, she saw another reflection, standing just behind her. She sucked in her breath.

It was her dad.

ten

Emergency!

Late Thursday Afternoon, July 10

Dad's face looked shocked. "Tess, what did you say?"

"It's true." Tess ducked out of the bathroom and around her dad. "I'm ugly." She started to cry. "I know it."

"Tess, that's not true."

"It *is* true, and I have proof." Tess ran down the hall.

"Proof?" her dad called after her.

"Please, Dad, just leave me alone." She hurried into her room and shut the door.

Her bed was a mess, her floor was a mess, and her desk was a mess. She couldn't even find a place to sit. Yanking open her closet door, she collapsed onto the carpet inside. She stared into the dark until her eyes adjusted, and she could see ghostlike clothes hanging all around her.

"I don't understand, Lord. I really don't know what to think. I'm very confused. I just want to be pretty. I want to look nice. I want to look like my mom, like Erin, like almost everyone else I know. But it looks as if I won't get to after all."

Scrunched up among the shoes, she placed her head on

her knees and let the tears slip down her cheeks. After a few minutes of sniffing, she heard her dad knock on her bedroom door.

"May I come in?" he asked.

Tess jumped out of the closet. She rubbed her eyes on the tomato red shirt sleeve and opened the door. "Okay," she said.

"Is there anywhere I can sit down?" Her dad surveyed the piles in the room.

Tess cleared a space on the bed, and they sat down together.

"What's the matter, honey?" he asked.

She twisted her hands in her lap. "I'm not as pretty as the other girls at the modeling school. I'm ugly."

"Tess, that's not true. It's really not. You're a lovely young lady."

Tess frowned. "You're my dad. You're supposed to say that. But today at the picture-taking, the photographer took a ton of pictures of Lila, who's this really cute girl, and Josie, who's really cute, too. And he even took a couple of extra ones of Erin!" She sniffled again. "But he only took five of me."

Tess's dad pulled her close. "And how many did he take of the other girls in the class?"

"I told you, lots!"

"Of all the girls, not just the three you told me about?"

Tess thought, chewing a hangnail. "Well, maybe he didn't take that many of all the girls."

"So how many did he take of the others, not just those three?"

Tess sighed. "Five, I guess."

"So five was the normal number?"

"I suppose so. But, Dad, I don't want to be normal. I want to be pretty."

Her dad touched her cheek. "You are pretty."

"But not as pretty as Mom," Tess shot back.

"When I look at you," he said, "I see a very pretty girl."

Tess smiled a little in spite of herself. "Dad, I could look like the Hunchback of Notre Dame, and you would say I was a pretty girl!"

"What makes you beautiful is that you're my daughter. When I look at you, I see the tiny baby you once were, and the young lady you are now, and all we have still to share. Do you understand?"

Don't get all cheesy, Tess thought. *It doesn't take away the plain truth.* But all she said was, "I guess so."

Her dad pointed to her shirt. "Better change. Your mom will be home soon. I know she's looking forward to taking you and Erin to the mall tonight to choose your outfits."

Tess stood up when he left. "All right." She closed the door behind him.

Dad tried, but he just didn't understand what she meant. She wanted to look a certain way, wanted people to think she was special. Wanted to be special. Calendar special. Lila special.

I guess I'd better pick up all Mom's stuff before she gets home. And find something to wear, she thought. She walked over to her dresser, opened the second drawer, and grabbed a short-sleeved shirt. She pulled off her mom's shirt and set it on top of the dresser, right next to the campus calendar. After putting on her shirt, she opened up her mom's calendar.

Tess flipped the pages to April. Her mom was so beautiful. Tess stared at her mother in the straw hat. *Someday I want to be like her, Lord.*

She set the calendar back down and noticed the calendar Erin had given her as a birthday gift beside it. *I haven't ripped off the pages for almost two weeks! I don't want Erin's feelings to be hurt if she stops by.* Snagging the day-by-day calendar off her desk, she began to rip the pages at July 1, then July 2. When she got to July 3, the word "beauty" caught her attention.

She ripped it off and read. "It is not fancy hair, gold jewelry, or fine clothes that should make you beautiful. No, your beauty should come from within you—the beauty of a gentle and quiet spirit. This beauty will never disappear, and it is worth very much to God (1 Peter 3:3-4)."

Did the Bible really say that?

She unzipped the denim Bible case Erin had given her, pulled out the Bible, and opened it. A piece of blue paper fluttered to the ground.

The modeling school flier. Tess had used it as a bookmark. Unfolding it again, she read, "Modeling class for girls! What is real beauty? We can help you find it—for keeps!"

The brochure distracted her, and she forgot the Bible. Instead, she closed her eyes and thought over the day. Erin *had* said the lighting looked good on Tess. She still was going to pick out her new outfit and her new lip gloss tonight. She knew what colors to buy. Besides, Picture Perfect Photography wasn't making the decision about modeling, Mr. Riggs was. And he was making that decision based on what happened at the store on Friday and on her working hard. She still had reason to hope!

When she opened her eyes, she licked her pointer finger and flipped through the Bible's thin pages, trying to find First Peter.

Suddenly she heard a shout in the hallway, "Tess, Tess, emergency!"

Tyler!

She jumped up, leaving the Bible on her bed, and ran to her door.

"What is it?" She flung open the door.

"It's Mom! She's in the hospital!"

eleven

The Waiting Game

Late Thursday Afternoon, July 10

Tess's chest tightened, and she couldn't take a deep breath. "Right now?"

"Right now!" Tyler said, panting.

"Does Dad know?"

"Of course Dad knows!" Tyler said.

"Is she having the baby?" Tess asked.

"I—I don't know." Tyler's eyes opened wide. "But I do know that Dad said something is wrong, and Mom couldn't even come home before going to the hospital!"

"Oh no, that doesn't sound good at all!" Tess ran down the hallway to her parents' room. "Is Mom okay?"

Her dad tossed some of her mother's makeup and other personal items into her already prepared suitcase. "Yes. She called me from the emergency room."

"Emergency room!" Tess felt dizzy. "I thought Tyler was kidding when he said it was an emergency."

"I think they're just checking her out there, then they'll give her a regular room in the maternity ward. Sometimes when pregnant mothers are older, their blood pressure goes up. It can be dangerous for the baby and for the mom. When Mom was at the doctor's office today, her blood pressure was too high. So they sent her in just to be safe."

"But Mom isn't old."

Her dad smiled. "No, she's not. And she'll be okay." Her dad snapped the suitcase shut. "I told Tyler to get his stuff prepared, and you need to do the same. I'm taking him to Big Al's and you to Erin's, and then I'm off to the hospital. Be ready in five minutes, okay?"

"All right." Tess flew back to her room and opened up her small suitcase. She tossed in some pajamas, a hairbrush, her makeup kit, a pair of shorts, and a T-shirt. She snapped her suitcase shut. Flipping off the light switch on the way out, she surveyed her room. Disaster. She would have to clean it when she got home. She stopped off at the bathroom and scrubbed the mascara off her face. Done.

"Are you ready?" she called to Tyler on her way down the hall.

"I'm already at the door," he answered. They locked up and headed out toward the garage, where their dad was putting their mom's suitcase into the trunk. Next in was Tess's suitcase, then Tyler's, then sleeping bags for both of them. A minute later, they were on their way.

As Tess stared out the window, she saw an ad for Robinson's-May on a billboard. "Dad, Mom was supposed to take us to the mall tonight!"

Her dad turned around and smiled at her. "Tess, something tells me that's just not going to happen."

"That's okay." The most important thing was her mom.

But Tess couldn't wear her shorts tomorrow, and Erin's clothes might not fit.

"Listen," her dad said, "Erin's mom will help out. When we pull into Big Al's driveway, I'll get some cash out of my wallet for your outfit." He saw the look on her face. "I'm sorry, but it will all work out. Your mom won't be able to watch you model tomorrow, but I can. Okay?"

That means if I do all right, Mr. Riggs will have to talk with Dad instead of Mom. Tess saw the earnest look on her father's face. He was trying, and she didn't want to hurt his feelings.

"Thanks, Dad."

When they pulled into Big Al's driveway, he came running out. "Hey, buddy, I have a new cartridge for us, come on!"

"'Bye, Tess," Tyler said. He held her hand for a minute. She squeezed it and kissed his cheek. "I'll see you soon."

Tyler hopped out of the Jeep, but his skin was milky white. "Dad, you'll call me tonight, won't you? And let me know Mom is okay?"

"Of course I will," his dad said. He went to the trunk to retrieve Tyler's suitcase and sleeping bag.

"Hey, I hear you're trying to be a model." Big Al leered in the Jeep window at Tess.

Tess rolled up the window while he was talking.

"I hear they might be looking for someone to play Big Foot. You have the huge feet, and you're hairy enough," he shouted.

"Pest," Tess shouted back. "And I'm not hairy." She finished rolling up the window and turned her back on him

A few minutes later her dad emerged from Big Al's house, ready to take her to Erin's.

"You'll call me, too, right, Dad?"

"Of course, cupcake. As soon as Mom is all settled in her room, and we know what's going on. But," he warned, "that may take some time. So don't worry, okay?"

"Okay," Tess's voice squeaked out.

They pulled up at Erin's house, and after her dad made sure Tess was okay, he took off for the hospital.

"Come on in," Erin's mother said. "We're just about ready to eat dinner. I'll bet you haven't eaten yet, have you?"

"No, I haven't. Thank you very much."

"Why don't you take Tess's stuff into your room, Erin, and we'll be eating in about"—Erin's mother checked the egg-shaped clock—"seven minutes."

After they were in Erin's room, Tess said, "We have a problem."

"You mean your mom does? I'm so sorry."

"I'm already worried enough about my mom, so don't tell me any horror stories, okay?" Tess snapped.

"Sorry," Erin whispered. "I wasn't going to tell you any horror stories."

Tess sat down on the bed. "I'm sorry, Erin. I didn't mean to freak out like that. I guess I'm really worried."

"Is that what the problem is?" Erin asked.

"Well, what I was talking about was the shopping trip." Tess kicked off her shoes. "Remember?"

"Oh yeah." Erin sat down next to Tess. "I'll ask my mom if she'll take us. My dad is at work, of course, so it depends on whether Tom can stay home with Josh. I'll ask at dinner."

"Oh. Your brothers are home?" Tess asked.

"Of course, silly," Erin said. "They do live here."

A few minutes later they were at the dinner table. Since Erin's dad was a chef, he wasn't home for dinner most nights.

"Tom, would you please ask the blessing?" Mrs. Janssen asked.

The steam carried a meaty, doughy smell from the casserole dish to Tess's nose.

"Lord, please bless this food to our bodies and help us to spend our energy doing things that please you," Tom prayed. "And please help Tess's mom to be safe, and their new baby, too. In Jesus' name, amen."

Tess smiled at him across the table. That was sweet of him to remember to pray for her mom.

After spooning in a few mouthfuls of Impossible Cheeseburger Pie, Erin spoke up. "Mom, since Tess's mother can't take us shopping tonight, would you be able to? We have to buy a few things at the drugstore and then our outfits for tomorrow."

"Sure," her mother answered. "Tom, can you please stay home with Josh?"

"All right," Tom agreed. "Are you two still modeling tomorrow?"

"Yes," Erin said sharply. She looked at him as if to say, Don't give us any guff.

"I just think you should spend time doing something that counts," he said.

"Like what?" Erin asked.

"Like, ah, I don't know," he answered. Then he ate another mouthful or two.

"Tess," he said, "don't you work in the nursery at church?"

"I did," Tess admitted, "but they asked me to move into working with the preschoolers."

"They asked her because she's so good with the kids," Erin bragged. Tess smiled at her friend.

"Great!" Tom said. "I knew you did important things. I respect that."

"Since when are you so interested in preschoolers?" Josh asked. Josh was going into fourth grade, like Tyler.

"Since I'm the youth leader in charge of Vacation Bible School at the Navajo mission next month. You are going, aren't you?" Tom asked Tess.

Tess swallowed some iced tea. "I think so. My parents didn't say yes yet." She looked up. "But I think they will."

"Then you'll help? Maybe with party planning. Or cleanup crew. You, too, Erin, okay?"

"For a price," Erin said.

Her mother laughed. "Oh, Erin, you can help."

"It sounds great." Tess ate a bit more, then set down her fork. She wished the phone would ring.

"Well, girls, we had better get going," Erin's mother said. "Before it gets too late. Boys, please clean up the dishes."

Josh groaned.

"I'll be ready in five minutes," Mrs. Janssen said, leaving the room.

I wish she would wait till my dad calls, Tess thought. *And they don't even have a cell phone.* But Erin's mom was already doing so much for Tess that she didn't feel she could ask Mrs. Janssen to wait.

twelve

The Call

Thursday Evening, July 10

"Do you want to go to the drugstore first to pick out the makeup or buy the clothes first?" Erin's mom asked.

"How about clothes?" Erin suggested. "That way we can pick out some lip gloss that matches."

"Good idea," Tess agreed. She took a deep breath and faced forward. No sense being worried for the next few hours. She couldn't do anything to help her mom anyway.

Erin's mother parked at Robinson's-May, and they walked into the junior department. "I'll just go look at the women's clothes for a few minutes, and I'll meet you back here in about a half-hour, okay?" she asked. Erin nodded, and her mom walked off.

"Should we look for you first or for me first?" Erin asked. "How about for you?"

Tess chewed on the soft flesh on the inside of her lip before answering. "Why don't we each pick out something we like and then meet in the dressing room?" She didn't want to hurry Erin, but she wanted to get back for her dad's call.

"Okay," Erin said. "I thought I saw something over here."

As soon as Erin left, Tess whipped out her color chart. First, she scouted for the peach shirt. She found it, but Mr. Riggs already had seen that shirt last week, and he didn't hire that model. What if he hated the shirt? A lot was riding on what outfit she chose.

She examined the shirt for a minute before tossing it over her arm. She would try it anyway.

She grabbed a pair of khakis and a brown woven belt. She also selected a pair of black boot-cut pants with a white T-shirt and a black vest.

A minute later, Erin's voice called all the way across the department, "Tess, where are you?"

"I'm here," Tess said. "I found some stuff, did you?"

"Yep!" Erin held out her arm. She had a light pink dress made of soft cotton. "I don't think many people will wear dresses, so I thought I'd pick one. It's not really something I'd wear to school, but I'll wear it to church."

As they walked into the dressing room, Erin said, "Hey, what if we buy fake motorcycle tattoos just to freak out Miss Wakested?"

"You're joking!" Tess said.

"I am." Erin giggled. "But I'd love to see her face! 'Motorcycle tattoos aren't ladylike, darling,'" she said, imitating Miss Wakested's voice.

Tess walked into the dressing room next to Erin's. It felt good to let the worry slip away for a minute and smile. Tess tried on the black-and-white outfit, and it looked okay. She checked her color chart. Black really wasn't one of her colors. It made her face look kind of washed out. Next she put on the khakis and the peach shirt. Much better.

"Well, what do you think?" she stepped out of the dressing room and in front of the mirror where Erin waited.

"I love it. I really do," Erin said. "But isn't that the exact same outfit that girl wore last week?"

"Yes," Tess admitted.

"What do you think of mine?" Erin asked. She twirled in the dress.

"It looks really nice," Tess said. "You look just like a real model."

They met Erin's mom at the cash register.

"Well, what did you find?" she asked.

Erin showed her the dress.

"As long as you'll wear it, it's okay," her mom said. "What are you getting, Tess?"

Tess looked at both of her outfits. First at the black and white. Then at the peach. Finally she pulled back her shoulders, lifted her head, and said, "I'm buying this one," holding up the peach shirt and khakis. She had learned what looked good on her, what she liked. And she liked this outfit.

After paying, they drove to the drugstore.

"The drugstore has a pay phone, doesn't it?" Tess asked.

"Do you want me to see if your dad has called our house?" Mrs. Janssen asked.

"Yes, please," Tess said. She and Erin walked to the cosmetics aisle.

"Will you help me find some blush that matches?" Tess asked.

After stroking several colors on the inside of Tess's wrist, as Miss Wakested had taught them, they found one that looked just right. Erin's mom appeared just as they were testing some on Erin.

"Did Dad call yet?" Tess asked.

Erin's mother shook her head. Tess's face fell.

"Don't worry," Mrs. Janssen said. "Sometimes it takes a long time to check into the hospital."

"Oh." Tess had a bitter taste in her mouth.

"Let's pick our lip gloss," Erin said. "Something really new, something that we've never had before. Something that says we're ready for junior high."

"Okay," Tess said. *Please, Lord, let my mom be okay. And the baby.*

"How about Dazzleberry?" Erin said. "What do you think?" She held up the tube.

"I like it."

"And now for you," Erin said. She seemed to notice Tess's drawn face. "Don't worry," she whispered. "Everything will be okay. Let's find one you like."

Tess smiled. Erin was right. This was as good a time as any to find something new and bold for junior high. And for tomorrow. Mom was surely okay.

They sorted through the rows of lip gloss. Nothing with glitter. Tess didn't want to look as if she had smeared frosting on her lips.

Back behind the tubes of Grape Kisses she spied just a snip of color. She couldn't quite see what it was called, but the color seemed just right for her. Tess moved some of the Grape Kisses packages off the rack and pulled out the one she wanted.

"What do you think?" She held it up for Erin to see.

"Perfect!" Erin said. "What color is it?"

Tess laughed as she read it. "Peaches and Cream!"

On the way back to Erin's house, Tess felt nervous again. It had been a couple of hours since her dad had dropped her off. Why hadn't he called? He knew she was worried.

Erin and her mother must have sensed Tess's concern

because nobody talked much on the way home. When they walked into the house, Tom was in the kitchen. He saw Tess's hopeful face and shook his head no.

Her heart dropped. What could be wrong?

She and Erin spent the evening ironing their outfits, and just before bedtime, the phone rang.

"I'll get it!" Tess said. "Oh." She looked at Erin with a smile. "I forgot it isn't my house."

Erin smiled back and picked up the phone before the third ring.

"Hello?" she asked. "Just a minute, please."

She handed the receiver to Tess.

"Hello?" Tess's voice quaked.

"Hi, Tess," her mother answered.

"Mom, how are you?"

"I'm just fine. They've brought me up to the maternity rooms, and they're just about to give me some very safe medicine that will speed up the baby's coming."

"Oh." Tess sighed. "I'm so glad you're okay! And is the baby okay?"

"They think so," her mother answered. "But just to be safe, they're going to make sure it's born soon."

"Soon," Tess said. *Soon!* she thought.

"Soon," her mother said with a laugh. "You go to sleep, and I'll bet that by the time you wake up tomorrow morning, we'll know whether you have a new brother or sister!"

thirteen

A Baby

Friday Morning, July 11

Tess tossed and turned all night on the family room floor where she and Erin slept. She had bad dreams and forgot where she was when she woke up in the night. Was the baby okay? And her mom? Would Tess stumble when she was modeling in front of all those people, including Mr. Riggs?

She was fully awake, though, the next morning when Erin's mom brought the phone into the family room. "Call for you!"

Rubbing her eyes into focus, Tess took the phone in her hand. "Hello?"

"Hi, Tess. This is Mom. We have a new baby!"

"We do? We do?" Tess said. "I mean, of course we do! Is it a boy or a girl?"

"A girl!" her mother said. "She was born early this morning, and she's just as healthy as can be."

"A girl!" Tess said. She jostled Erin. "It's a healthy baby girl."

"Dad is going to pick up Tyler and you," Tess's mother

said. "He'll bring you both over to the hospital for a visit. Then he and Tyler will go to Robinson's-May to watch you model. Okay?"

"Okay!" Tess said. The baby was okay, but what about her mother? She held her breath. "Mom?"

"Yes?"

"How are you? I mean, are you fine? Are you really okay?"

"Of course, I'm just fine. Why?"

Tess felt her smile reach both earlobes. "Just wondering. See you soon. I love you."

"I love you, too." Her mother sounded weary but well.

Tess clicked off the phone and handed it back to Erin's mother. Then Tess grabbed Erin's hands and danced around the room. "Woooee! This is great!"

Erin pulled her hands away. "So you have a sister."

"Yes, isn't that great? A healthy girl, and my mom is okay. Everything is great!"

"Great," Erin said.

Tess stared at her. Erin wasn't acting as if everything was great. Maybe she was worried about modeling later.

Tess knelt down to roll up her sleeping bag. "My dad is picking up Tyler, and then he'll be here for me. We're going to the hospital for a little while, but I'll meet you at the store." Her heart trembled as she thought about modeling. One good thing had already happened today. Maybe there could be another!

"Do you know what?" Tess jumped up. "I forgot to ask what they named my sister. And my mom was so tired she forgot to tell me!" She giggled. "I'll ask when I get there. I hope it's not Gertrude. They said they were going to name her Gertrude, if it was a girl, but I think they were just kidding."

Tess and Erin carried their sleeping bags into Erin's room, and then Tess packed her clothes for their very first modeling assignment.

"I don't want anything to get wrinkled," she explained, "while I'm holding my sister or anything."

At breakfast, Erin ignored her cereal then walked Tess to the door as Tess's dad pulled up.

Tess hugged her. "I'll see you in about two hours, okay?"

"Okay," Erin said.

As soon as Tess walked into the hospital, she noticed big rainbow bouquets of balloons and flowers sitting on the reception desk, waiting to be delivered. *We should have bought something for Mom.* Then the elevator took so long to get there. But finally they found her mom's room.

"Hi, Mom!" Tess said as she walked in. Her mother looked terrific. Tess smiled in relief.

Their mother sat up in bed, a thin blue hospital gown pulled around her. "Hi, guys. Come here and look at your new sister."

Tyler walked up first and shyly peeked at the bundle in his mother's arms. The baby was all rolled up like a tiny pink egg roll with a soft knitted cap on her head.

A wave of warmth filled Tess from the center of her body out to her arms and legs. This was *her* sister. Forever. "What's her name?" Tess moved closer.

"Tara," her mother answered. Then she sipped water from a big cup next to her bed. "Would you like to hold her?"

"No, um, not yet," Tyler said. "She's pretty small. I—I might do it at home."

"Okay," their mom said. "Tess?"

"Yes," Tess said. Tara. What a pretty name for a pretty girl.

"I'll bring the baby to her, Molly," Tess's dad said. "You rest." He picked up the baby and carried her over to Tess. "Sit down, okay?"

Tess sat, held out her arms, and nestled the baby close to her.

She stared at the baby's face. Tara's nose was cute, and her little eyes were squeezed shut. But a big red-and-purple spot was on her cheek. It looked like a bruise. Something was wrong.

"Mom?" Tess took a deep breath. "What's wrong with her face?"

Tess saw her mother and father exchange glances. Then Tess looked at Tyler, and she could tell he had been thinking the same thing.

"Nothing is wrong, Tess. Tara has a birthmark. Some people call it a wine stain, but the doctor who helped deliver her called it an 'angel kiss,' which sounds nicer. It doesn't hurt her."

"Will it go away?" Tyler rushed in.

"Maybe, maybe not. It will lighten a little bit, but unless she has laser surgery to remove it when she gets older, it will probably always be there."

"Oh." At least her mom and the baby were healthy. And Tess had a sister. It's just that, well, Tess wasn't expecting this, that's all.

"Now I have a big girl and a little girl," her dad said.

"Dad, please don't start calling me a big girl," Tess said. They all laughed.

The noise must have startled Tara because her eyes flew open, and she looked right into Tess's eyes.

"Hi, little sister," Tess whispered.

Tara stared right back but didn't cry.

"I think she likes you," her mother said.

"Hey, my turn!" Tyler said.

"I thought you didn't want to hold her?" their dad teased.

"A chap's allowed to change his mind, isn't he?" Tyler said.

Tyler and Tess switched places.

"Was Erin excited about the baby?" Her mother faced Tess expectantly.

Tess stopped to think. Then she frowned. "You know, she didn't say."

Her dad checked his watch. "You had better hurry up and get changed. We only have a half-hour before we go to meet the Impressive Miss Wakested and the Important Mr. Riggs."

fourteen

Modeling Show

Friday, July 11

The junior department was crowded again, just like last week. But this time it was Tess's big moment. She hid her hands so no one would see her bitten nails.

"Tyler and I will stand over here, okay?" Tess's dad said. He pointed to a relatively free space near the end of the aisle, which had been turned into a runway. "I'll be able to take good movies from here." He held up his video recorder.

Tess rolled her eyes. Her mother had insisted, since she couldn't be there, that Tess's dad tape it.

"Okay. I think I have to go over by the rest of the class," Tess said. "I'll come and stand by you when it's over."

Tess walked over to the counter where Miss Wakested and the other girls were. Erin wasn't there yet.

But Mr. Riggs was. He had squeezed into the same leather chair he had sat in during last week's modeling session and had a stack of photos from Picture Perfect Photography on his lap.

"Tess, you look lovely," Miss Wakested said. "Is your friend Erin here yet?" She ran her shiny nails through her hair.

"I don't see her. But I'm sure she'll be here soon."

Miss Wakested nodded and turned her attention to someone else.

"Tess!" Lila ran over to her. "You look fantastic. That color is so good on you."

"Thanks," Tess said. She looked Lila up and down. "And you look like, well, you look like a real model."

"Oh. Well, Miss Wakested made me change. It was so strange. I had on what I thought was a great outfit, but as soon as I got here, she made some strange clicking noises. Then she dragged me and my mom into the dressing room and handed this to me."

"I don't know what you had on before, but that dress is great."

Lila smiled, her perfect teeth lighting up the whole area. "Thanks. I guess melon is one of my colors. Hey, there's Josie. I'm going to stand by her. But I wanted to tell you thanks for being so nice to me this week." She waved to Josie. "See you later, Tess."

Tess looked around. Almost everyone had on dresses. *Where is Erin?*

A voice came from behind her. "Hi, Tess."

"Yikes!" Tess turned around. "You scared me to death!" She hugged Erin. "I'm so glad you're here. I was starting to worry. It's almost time to start!"

Erin nodded.

"Ladies, let's meet at the end of the runway, please," Miss Wakested called from the side. The class lined up behind the announcer, and the crowd grew silent. Tess peeked around the counter and saw Tyler and her dad, video camera whirring.

"I'm afraid this will be recorded for eternity, good or bad!" she whispered to Erin.

Erin smiled back.

Miss Wakested took the microphone. "Thank you all for coming today to support our lovely models on their first assignment. We'll announce the girls by name and the clothes they've chosen, and then they will model down the aisle and back again." She sipped out of a paper cup before continuing.

"I'd like to introduce our honored guest, Jason Riggs. Mr. Riggs is a principal in the Brownstone, Riggs, and Johnson Modeling Agency of Los Angeles. He's talent scouting and shooting some commercials here in Arizona. After the program, he may wish to speak to one or more of the girls and their parents about other modeling possibilities."

She turned to the class and put her hand over the microphone. "Ready, girls?" Annalise, who was to model first, nodded.

Miss Wakested handed the microphone to the announcer, who had each girl's name and outfit on a piece of paper.

Annalise was first, then Jamie. Next was Erin.

"Go, Erin!" Tess whispered. "I'm rooting for you!"

Erin walked down the runway, wobbling on her heels at first but then more surefooted. Tess watched as even Tom smiled when Erin walked by. The dress was great, and with her hair down Erin looked more impressive than ever. Tess noticed that Mr. Riggs stared the whole time and didn't consult his pictures until Erin was back at Tess's side.

"How did I do?" Erin whispered.

"Great, just great!" Tess said. Her stomach felt heavy, like a ball of oatmeal sat inside. "I don't want to talk till my turn is over though. I'm kind of nervous."

Erin nodded. After two more girls, it was Tess's turn.

The announcer called out his information as Tess walked down the aisle. "Ladies and gentlemen, I'd like to introduce Tess Thomas. She's wearing a light cotton-silk blended shirt paired with side-pocket khakis. Her belt, too, can be found in the junior department. All this week at Robinson's-May."

Tess held up her head. She felt older, more sophisticated. Not pretty, but confident, together. She smiled at Mr. Riggs, and he smiled back. *He smiled at me! I'm glad I wore what I wanted to wear, trusted myself.*

Then she smiled at her dad, who grinned back. Tyler whistled.

The announcer finished, "Let's give a big round of applause for Tess Thomas!"

There was just as much applause for Tess as for anyone else.

She walked back to where Erin waited.

"Did I look okay?" she asked.

"Great," Erin said.

A few other girls from the class modeled and then Lila.

"Ladies and gentlemen, I'd like to introduce Lila Nelson." The announcer went on to tell about Lila's dress.

Tess tuned him out. She could barely take her eyes off Lila, who looked so beautiful and confident. Tess glanced at Mr. Riggs. He, too, was staring. Lila's mom, a tall blonde like her daughter, watched from the sidelines. Lila was together, sophisticated, and confident. And she also was beautiful.

Afterward, a cookies-and-punch reception took place in the junior department. Miss Wakested talked to some of the girls, and Mr. Riggs did, too. Unsure of what to do while waiting to hear from Mr. Riggs, Tess and Erin walked around with their families for a while, then sat down to eat cookies.

"They named the baby Tara," Tess said.

"That's neat," Erin said. "Did you get to hold her? Aren't you glad there's nothing wrong with her, that's she a beautiful, perfect baby?"

Tess gulped. She wasn't ready to talk about the angel kiss with anyone right now. Not even Erin.

"Yeah," Tess said.

"Well, I'll get to see her for myself tomorrow," Erin said. "Your *sister,* that is."

Tess's eyes opened wide. "What do you mean?"

"My mom is bringing over some food for you guys, and I want to come, too, of course, and see her." She looked at Tess's troubled face. "You don't want me to come?"

"Of course I want you to come. It's just—"

At that moment Miss Wakested walked up. "You did a great job, girls, and I enjoyed having you in class."

"Thank you," Tess said.

"Well, I wish you the best of luck!" Miss Wakested held out her hand.

Erin shook it first, then Tess.

"Is that, ah, all?" Tess asked. She looked over Miss Wakested's shoulder, trying to locate Mr. Riggs. She spied him, deep in conversation with Lila and her mother.

"Were you expecting something else?" Miss Wakested asked.

"No, I guess not." Tess forced back tears. So she hadn't

been chosen after all. Even though she looked great in the outfit she had chosen with the matching Peaches and Cream lip gloss. And she hadn't stumbled or anything. And she had worked really hard, just like Mr. Riggs had said.

"I guess I'll go find my dad." Tess turned her back to Miss Wakested.

"Tess," Miss Wakested called out as Tess began to walk away. "Wait!"

fifteen

Family of Five

Friday evening, July 11; Saturday morning, July 12

Tess turned around.

"I just want to tell you that you did a fine job. I saw how hard you worked," Miss Wakested said.

"Thanks," Tess said as her dad walked up. "Are you ready to go, Dad?" Tess smiled weakly as Miss Wakested left. Erin had wandered off, and she seemed mad at Tess anyway. Right now Tess just wanted to go home.

"Sure, sure," he said. "Are you ready?" He looked in the direction of Mr. Riggs and then back at Tess.

Tess's lip quivered. "There's no reason to stay now," she said. *Please don't make me say it aloud.*

"Okay, cupcake," he said.

Tess sighed. *It's pretty clear after today that I'm a plain vanilla cupcake. Even though I wanted to be strawberry supreme.*

Tyler reached his arm around her. "I say, you did a great job, old cork. I thought you were much prettier than those other girls."

Tess looked down at his earnest face and grinned in spite of herself. "Thanks."

Her dad reached over and took her hand, and the three of them walked out to the car. "Let's get the place ready for the baby to come home."

And Erin was coming over tomorrow. Probably.

The next morning, they went to the hospital to take Mrs. Thomas and Tara home.

"I hope she likes her room," Tyler said as they pulled into the garage.

"Like she'll even know!" Tess teased.

"I helped paint it," he said. "So she should."

Their dad shut off the car, and Tyler ran into the house. "I have to see if Big Al left me a message. He's reached a new level on Game Boy, and he said he would call me with the password."

Tess rolled her eyes. "Can I help you with something, Mom?" Tess grabbed the diaper bag on the way in.

"No, honey, I'm just going to feed the baby, put her in her cradle for a nap, and then close my eyes for a few minutes. Erin will be here soon. Why don't you clean up your room before she gets here?" Her mother winked. "Unless you've already done it. Which I doubt."

"Nah, it's not done." She kissed her mom on the cheek and Tara on her cheek. But not the cheek with the spot.

"I'll come out and get the door when I hear Erin pull up. I want to let them in first, okay? And then I'll bring Erin to see the baby after a while."

"All right." Her mom wandered into the family room and sank onto the couch.

Tess walked to her room. *Oh, man, no way can I clean this up in a few minutes!*

She started at her desk, shoving a whole bunch of leaky pens and eraserless pencils into the top drawer. She tried to pick a wad of stuck gum off the desk's top.

Might as well start with the messy bulletin board. It's the easiest job here. She walked over to it and ripped off the modeling school flier. "Do you want real beauty?" she read again.

She felt the tears and closed her eyes. *Lord, I want you to know that I'm not upset about Lila. She's really nice. So it's okay that she got to talk with Mr. Riggs. But even though I'm not mad anymore, I do feel sad. I wanted to model. I really did. I guess Tom was right. I'll never be a real model.*

Some of Tom's other words floated back to her. "You do important things," he had said, talking about her work with the kids at church. "I respect that."

She smiled, just a little. There *were* other things to be admired for besides being pretty.

As she opened her eyes, she caught sight of the family picture she had tacked up the night she had helped her mom clean out the baby's closet.

A family of four—Mom, Dad, Tess, and Tyler—all decked out in fancy clothes. But something already felt wrong with the picture.

"We're not a family of four anymore." She untacked the photo from the bulletin board and stared at it. It felt disloyal to Tara to have it up there, even though Tara wouldn't know enough to have hurt feelings about it. But Tess did.

She let the picture flutter into the open drawer. "We're a family of five now."

The next piece of paper tacked up was the calendar page from July 2. "It is not fancy hair, gold jewelry, or fine clothes that should make you beautiful. No, your beauty should come from within you—the beauty of a gentle and quiet spirit. This beauty will never disappear, and it is worth very much to God (1 Peter 3:3-4)."

She left the verse on the board and opened her heart, letting in a steady trickle of truth about what real beauty was. It began to wash away her false understanding. *I want your kind of beauty, Lord.*

She heard Erin's Suburban pull into the driveway.

"I'll get the door!" She skidded out of her room and down the hallway and opened the front door.

"Here she is, the big sister!" Erin's mother called out as she shut the car door. "Can you help us carry in the food?"

Erin said nothing. She didn't even look Tess in the eye.

Tess slipped into her sandals and ran down the oven-hot driveway. "Wow, is all of this for us?"

"I wanted to set you up for a few days," Erin's mother said. "So your mom can rest."

Into the kitchen they lugged frozen casseroles, cold salads, and bags of rolls. Tess balanced a huge Tupperware container stuffed with chocolate-chip cookies on top of her head, walking like an African queen.

"Where's your mom?" Mrs. Janssen asked.

"She's in the family room," Tess said. She walked them into the room. "Erin's here," she called to her mother. "We're going to my room."

"But, Tess," Erin finally spoke as Tess walked past the baby's room and into her bedroom. "I want to see the baby."

"I know, I know," Tess said. "We will. Let's let your mom go first."

"Can't we all go at once?"

"Well, we could, but…"

Erin sat down on Tess's bed. "What's the problem?"

Tess sat down next to her. She could hear Mrs. Janssen across the hall quietly cooing over Tara.

"I'll take you over there in a minute. But don't say anything bad, okay?"

"Bad?" Erin's face screwed up. "What do you mean?"

"Well, Tara has a, uh, thing."

"Thing?"

Tess looked at her hands. "She has a birthmark on her face. A big red spot. They call it an angel kiss."

"Oh, okay. Why would I say anything bad?" Erin stood up. "I'm not that rude."

"No, I know you're not. I mean, don't be mad!" Tess said. "I—I don't know. It was just a surprise."

"Yeah, I can understand that." Erin looked right at Tess. "Are you embarrassed about her?"

"No!"

They heard the mothers talking as they walked back down the hall. They weren't with the baby anymore.

"We can go in now." Tess opened her door, and together they tiptoed into Tara's room.

Erin peeked into the cradle on one side, and Tess peeked in on the other, watching Baby Tara's chest rise and fall as she slept.

The blinds were pulled shut so the baby could sleep, and on the light blue walls glowing yellow stars were scattered about. Inside the dresser drawers neat piles of tiny T-shirts, soft towels, and fuzzy booties waited for the baby too. A pink bottle of creamy lotion sat on top of the dresser, and in the corner of the room was a tiny tub for sponge baths.

"She's so pretty," Erin said. She held up a teddy bear. "I brought her a present."

"Thanks," Tess said. "Do you really think she's pretty? I do, but then, I'm her sister." Tess sat down in the rocking chair.

"Sister," Erin said flatly.

Tess looked at her. "Is something wrong?"

"Well, I've been meaning to talk to you about that." Erin never took her eyes off Tara. "I mean, you have a real sister now. You don't need me to be your sister anymore." Erin looked at Tara, not Tess, but Tess could see tears fill Erin's eyes.

Tess stood up. "Erin, you will always be my real sister, too. We'll *both* be big sisters to Tara. And she's little, I mean, it's not like she can hang out with me or anything." She hugged Erin, and Erin hugged her back.

"I'm so glad we're still sisters," Erin said.

Tara started to cry. Tess reached into the cradle and lifted the baby out, careful to put one hand under the baby's neck and head. Tara stopped crying right away.

"Say, scaring the baby?" Tyler glanced into the room.

"No, I'm taking her to Mom."

Tyler suddenly stopped and turned around.

"Hey, I forgot to tell you. When I was on the phone with Big Al, your friend Lila called. I was in a really important discussion, so I told her you would call her back. She said it was very important."

"Oh, I wonder what it could be. Where did you write down her number?" Tess asked.

Tyler said nothing, backing down the hall.

"Did you get her number?" Tess demanded, not wanting to chase after him with the baby in her arms. Asking for phone numbers was a family rule. "Because I don't have it. Did you?"

"I thought you already had it, so I didn't ask." He dashed into his room and slammed the door shut.

"Sorry!" he shouted from the other side.

sixteen

Important Call #2

Saturday Afternoon, July 12

After Erin and her mother left, Tess tried to call Miss Wakested to get Lila's number. No one answered. Tess looked up "Nelson" in the Scottsdale phone book. Too many to call. And what if Lila lived in nearby Phoenix or Mesa?

Why would Lila call her? What could be "very important"? Tess sighed and left the phone book in the kitchen. "Might as well check on the baby."

When she walked into Tara's room, her mother was sitting in the rocking chair, holding the baby.

"I'd like to take a quick shower, and Dad is napping. Do you want to rock the baby for a while?"

"I don't know," Tess said. "What if she cries?"

"Walk her around for a minute or two. If she doesn't quiet down, come and knock on my door. I won't be long," her mom promised.

"All right. But wait just a minute! I forgot something I wanted to give Tara. I wanted to put it in her room before she came home, but everything happened so fast I forgot."

"What—" her mother started, but Tess was on her way down the hall.

Opening the door to her room, Tess made her way over to the little trunk in the corner. She opened the lid and found what she was looking for. Unrolling the protective cotton blanket, she took out her Baby Dimples.

"Hi," she whispered to the doll. Dimples's eyes were closed, so Tess held her up, and they opened automatically. After first making sure that no one was looking in from the hall, she cuddled Baby Dimples close.

"I know I haven't brought you out for a long while, not since the beginning of the year," Tess continued. Last September, with her world tumbling all around her, Tess had told all her secrets to her long-loved doll. But since then, she had had God and Erin, and so her doll had stayed tucked neatly away.

"Anyway, I have an important job for you," she said. "I know I said I'd never give you away. And I'm not, really. But I think it's time for someone new to love you."

Still clutching the doll, she made her way back into Tara's room.

"What's that?" her mother asked. Then she saw Baby Dimples.

"Oh, Tess, are you giving her to Tara?"

Tess nodded as she placed Baby Dimples on Tara's dresser. Then Tess sat down in the rocking chair.

Her mother gently placed Tara in Tess's arms. Then her mom folded them both in a big hug. "My sweet girls." She kissed Tess's temple before leaving the room. "I'll be back soon."

Tess stared down at Tara, sleeping in her arms. Love flooded Tess's heart like warm water, overflowing into her spirit as Tara's fingers curled around Tess's. "I never would have imagined that I'd have a real baby to hold," she whispered. Carefully, slowly, she lifted her left pointer finger and touched the angel kiss for the first time.

"I'm sorry I was kind of yucky about this," she said. "Erin asked me if I was embarrassed about it. I don't think so. I'm not sure."

She caressed the baby's fine, soft hair with her open palm. "I think mostly I was afraid that other people will make fun of you. Will make you feel ugly. Because some people only look at the outside kind of beauty. But I know you're not ugly. I know you're beautiful."

Eyes still closed, Tara sucked on her tiny pink Binky, and it moved up and down in short spurts, popping out every few seconds. Tess kept putting it back in.

She smiled, remembering the things her dad had said only a few days before. Now she knew he had told the truth, and she understood what he had meant. Tess repeated his words now to Tara and meant them from the center of her own heart. "What makes you beautiful is that you are my sister," she whispered. "When I look at you I see the tiny baby you are, and the young lady you will be, and all we have still to share."

Tess continued, "You are my sister. I can't wait to do things together, share treasures." She looked over at Baby Dimples, sitting on the dresser, then back at Tara.

"And I know God, and I can teach you about him. Nothing is too good for you; I'll always protect you. Because even if you never get your angel kiss removed, you will always be picture perfect to me."

She bent down and kissed the bright red spot on Tara's cheek.

"Are you doing okay?" Her mother walked into the room, damp hair hanging around her shoulders as she pulled her bathrobe tightly about her.

Tess stood up, startled. "Mom, that was so fast!"

"I worried about leaving you for too long. I knew you were nervous."

I wonder if she heard what I was saying, Tess thought. *Not that it was anything bad, just, well, private.*

Her mother gave no indication that she had overheard. "What were you and Tyler fighting about?" Her mom eased the baby from Tess's arms and nursed her in the rocking chair. Tess sat on the floor next to them.

"Lila called me, but Tyler forgot to save the number."

"I'm sure she'll call back."

"I'm sure she won't." Tess folded her hands together. "She's going to think I ignored her. She'll think that I'm mad because Mr. Riggs talked to her and not to me."

"Are you mad about that? I know how much you wanted to be a model."

Tess picked at a hangnail. "Well, I was disappointed for a lot of reasons. One of them was that I wanted to be a model, to be as beautiful as you."

Her mother looked down at Tess with soft eyes but said nothing.

"But I'm not mad," Tess continued. "Lila is a pretty girl. She deserved it."

"You're a pretty girl, too," her mother said.

Tess pursed her lips, thinking. "Well, maybe not pretty. I'm normal looking." There, she had said it aloud. And it felt okay. She smiled.

Quietness passed between them. Tess raveled the edge

of the baby blanket that hung over the rocking chair's arm and tickled her leg.

"I've learned a lot about real beauty though," Tess said. "From the Bible. From Dad." She stood up and kissed her sister's tiny hand, resting on their mother's arm. "And from Tara."

"You know, Tess," her mother said, "you said you wanted to be more like me. But in many ways, I want to be more like you. You've changed over the past year. You're special, beautiful inside in a way I don't think I am. Maybe you have some things to teach me."

Tess hugged her mother in silence for a second or two until Tyler burst into the room. "Hey, telephone!"

seventeen

Count Me In

Saturday Afternoon, July 12

"For who?" Tess asked.

Tyler covered the receiver with his hand. "For you."

Tess raced over and snatched the phone from him. She stepped out into the hallway. "Hello?"

"Hi, Tess, it's Lila."

"Oh hi, Lila. I'm so glad you called back! My brother forgot to get your number."

"It's okay. I just wanted to talk to you before anyone else called you."

Tess frowned. "What do you mean?"

"Like, Mr. Riggs."

Tess's eyes opened wide, and still holding the phone, she walked into her bedroom and closed the door behind her. "Why would Mr. Riggs call me?"

"Well," Lila said, "it's like this. I was in his office this morning, and he was talking to me about modeling jobs. My mom and I were sitting there, and his secretary knocked on the door. She came in and told him he had a very important visitor."

"And then?" Tess asked.

"So he asked my mom and me if we would mind waiting for a minute while he talked with this guy. We said no, we didn't mind. He rents this really big office when he's in Phoenix. Anyway this lady comes in and starts talking about how the Pizza Pronto owner has changed his mind and wants Mr. Riggs to find some girls for the commercial after all."

"But what does that have to do with me?" Tess asked.

"Just wait," Lila continued. "Mr. Riggs says, well, now I have to assemble a crowd of girls in just a few days. They wanted the commercial to be a bunch of girls eating pizza after a soccer game. He told his secretary to find some girls from the pictures of Miss Wakested's classes this summer. She was about to leave the room when I decided something."

Tess breathed faster. *I wish I had some water, my mouth is so dry.*

"I got really brave and said to Mr. Riggs, 'Well, two girls were in my class who would be great.' And then I told him your name and Erin's, and he went and looked through the Picture Perfect photos and showed them to the lady. She said, 'Terrific! Make sure these two are a part of whatever group you assemble.' So I thought they might call and offer you the job."

Tess's bed squeaked and sagged as she flopped down in the center of it. "He hasn't called. Maybe I'm not special enough, too normal."

"Not at all!" Lila said. "You're special, both on the outside and on the inside. You're different than a lot of other girls, in a good way. That's why I remembered you. You were so kind to me; I hope I can help you out this way. I hope Mr. Riggs calls you. I know he's busy, but he wanted to start shooting this commercial next week. He's going back to L.A. after that."

"Thanks," Tess said. "I really appreciate it. Will you be in the commercial, too?"

"No, he's sending me to L.A. for a day of photo shoots next week," Lila said. "Gotta go. Hope it all works out okay."

"'Bye," Tess said. She clicked off the phone and set it down next to her.

Could this be happening? Could it be true?

She clicked the phone on again, ready to call Erin. But what if Mr. Riggs never called? Then Erin would be disappointed all over again. Tess clicked off the phone.

She opened her door and went to tell her mother what had happened.

"So," Tess said, "if he calls, can I do it?"

"Well, if it's quick, and Erin's mom can stay there with you, I think it would be okay." Her mother smiled. "But let's see if he calls."

Tess went back to her room and cleaned like crazy to keep her mind off the possible phone call. When the phone did ring, she almost screamed.

Taking a deep breath, she answered it. "Hello?"

"Hello, may I speak with Tess Thomas?" a man's voice said.

"This is she."

"This is Jason Riggs, Miss Wakested's friend. I have a modeling job here in Phoenix next week, and you and your friend were recommended to me. The job would be one time and would pay $100 for two hours of work, plus a pizza a week for an entire year."

"Wonderful!" Tess said.

She jotted down the information Mr. Riggs gave her and said she would talk with her parents and then call him back. When she hung up, she started to dial Erin's number, then thought she would wait a minute in case Mr. Riggs tried to call Erin next.

She sat on her bed in silence for a few minutes, letting it all sink in. "Thank you, God, for letting my mom and Tara be safe. Thanks for Lila. And thank you for having Mr. Riggs call me. I guess I don't mind being plain vanilla, Lord," she whispered. "Because I know I'll always be strawberry supreme to you."

Opening her eyes, she picked up the phone and dialed Erin's number.

Have More Fun!!

Visit the official website at:
www.secretsisters.com

There are lots of activities and exciting new things to see!
If you don't have access to the Internet, please write to
me at:

Sandra Byrd
P.O. Box 2115
Gresham, OR 97030

Would you like to own your own Secret Sisters charms?
You can buy a set that includes each of the eight silver
charms Tess and Erin own—a heart, ponies, star, angel,
Bible, paintbrush, dolphin, and flower bouquet. Please
send $8 (includes shipping and handling) to: Parables
Charms, P.O. Box 2115, Gresham, OR 97030. Quantities
are limited.

Secret Sisters Photo Album

You'll need:

Two small photo albums that hold 4" x 6" pictures
A camera
Some film
Two plain 4" x 6" index cards

First, write each of your names, ages, and personal descriptions on the two index cards (brown hair, blue eyes, etc.). Write: "What we liked in sixth grade" (or whatever grade you're in). Slip a card into the first page of each photo album.

Next, take pictures of each other in different clothes that you really like—some Sunday-best outfits, some jeans-and-sweatshirts outfits. Take pictures of activities you like—your pet, your horse, your sport. Make silly faces and have someone take pictures of the two of you together. Have the film developed (double prints) and slip the pictures into the album sleeves—some of you, some of your Secret Sister in each album. You'll both always remember what you looked like, what you liked to wear that particular year, and that you did fun things together.

Did you like what you read? Then take a look At what will happen inside the next book.

Across

2 Erin's brother

4 The name of the youth pastor at Living Water Community Church

5 Lambs

6 Wrote the book Philippians in the New Testament

9 Humiliated

12 Not a lake or a stream but a…

Down

1 When one uses water in a ceremony to identify with Jesus' death and resurrection

3 Error

7 Distress, danger

8 An American Indian tribe whose reservation is in parts of Arizona and New Mexico

10 Something to keep hush-hush between just a few people, or perhaps no one knows but you

11 What kids do when Erin watches them

13 Stands for Vacation Bible School

#8 *Petal Power:* Ms. Martinez is the most beautiful bride in the world, and the sisters are there to help her get married. When trouble strikes her honeymoon plans, Tess and Erin must find a way to help save them.

#9 *First Place:* The Coronado Club insists Tess won't be able to hike across the Grand Canyon and plans to tell the whole sixth grade about it at Outdoor School. Tess looks confident but worries in silence, not wanting to share the secret that could lead to disaster.

#10 *Camp Cowgirl:* The Secret Sisters are ready for an awesome summer camp at a Tucson horse ranch, until something—and someone—interferes. What happens if your best friend wants other friends, and you're not sure, but you might too?

#11 *Picture Perfect:* Tess and Erin sign up for modeling school, but will they be able to go? Could they ever get any modeling assignments? Along the way the Secret Sisters find out that things aren't always just as they seem, a fact confirmed when Tess's mother has her baby.

#12 *Indian Summer:* When Tess and Erin sign up to go on their first mission trip—to the Navajo reservation—they plan to work at Vacation Bible School. What do a young Navajo girl and Tess have in common? In the end Tess has to make some of the most important choices in her new Christian life.

The Secret Sister Handbook: 101 Cool Ideas for You and Your Best Friend! It's fun to read about Tess and Erin and just as fun to do things with your own Secret Sister! This book is jam-packed with great things for you to do together all year long.